THE MIRACLE OF MERRIFORD

THE MIRACLE OF MERRIFORD

By REGINALD ARKELL

ILLUSTRATED BY
J. S. GOODALL

REYNAL & COMPANY, NEW YORK

THE MIRACLE OF MERRIFORD

SPRING HAD COME to Merriford, England. Ernie Mutlow's tortoise had woke up; old Mrs. Boulton's Scottie was chasing an early butterfly and the aconites in the Vicarage shrubbery were a fair picture.

You could always tell when Spring had come to Merriford by the aconites in the Vicarage shrubbery. There never was such a sight: a yellow carpet like that Field of the Cloth of Gold they told about in the history books.

It was the leaf mold that did it. Every year the

leaves fell from the nut bushes, and, as nobody bothered to sweep them up, the ground became all soft and spongy, like walking on a feather bed. No matter how hard the winter, the Vicarage shrubbery floor was always as soft as a feather bed—which was good for the aconites.

Every January you could see their bended necks pushing through the soft soil. Then, when they straightened up, there were the little yellow flowers with their green ruffs, such as were worn in the days of the first Queen Elizabeth.

Nobody walked in the Vicarage shrubbery any more; it was too much of a tangle. Thrushes and blackbirds nested in the laurels; small boys slipped through holes in the hedge to play at Indians, and, in the Autumn, the little grey squirrels had a high old time among the overgrown nut bushes. Then in January the aconites spread themselves out like a yellow carpet, and everything started all over again.

It hadn't always been like that. Fifty years ago, when the new parson brought his young wife to Merriford, the paths were kept clear and there were no holes in the hedges. The nuts were harvested, stored in large earthenware jars to last all the winter, and if the squirrels got more than their fair share they were lucky.

The shrubbery was not then the sanctuary for

small boys and birds that it had since become, but it *was* a sanctuary for the young couple who took the problems of their new and rather frightening position to its quiet walks and pleasant solitudes. Here they could throw off those embarrassing restraints that made a parish priest and his young wife seem so different to ordinary people in the eyes of their little world.

One of the odd things about being a country clergyman, they soon discovered, was that you were not supposed to share the trivial little setbacks and difficulties of your parishioners. Nobody stopped to wonder whether you had trouble with your old kitchen range or if you had enough money in the bank to pay your tradesmen's bills. They envied you your fine big house, ranked you socially next to the Squire, and reckoned you were lucky having to work only one day in the week.

So that in those old days, what with a young parson new to his job and a young wife new to *her* job, the Vicarage shrubbery had heard many confidences that would have surprised the good people of Merriford more than a little.

But that was all a long time ago. Today, looking at the overgrown shrubs and the holes in the hedges you might be tempted to say: "Another old parson lurking behind his evergreens! Old and cranky and past his job. . . . No good to anybody. . . . Trouble is they can't sack him . . . not even his bishop. . . . No wonder the churches are empty!"

THE VICAR of Merriford, now nearing his eight-ieth year, sat in his study wrestling with the *Times* crossword puzzle. But things weren't going too well with him.

What could one make, for instance, of "A plant with a kick in it (9)." This was one of those difficult mornings when nothing seemed to go right. Perhaps Mary could help him. He rang the little handbell on his desk and the study door was opened by a young girl, pretty as a picture, carrying a brush in one hand and a dustpan in the other.

"Mary!" said the Reverend. "What is a plant with a kick in it?"

Mary pretended to ponder the problem. The Reverend liked to have his little joke and she had to humor him. But she had never been kicked by a plant. Also, she had to keep an eye on the oven and the beds weren't made yet.

"Why don't you put it away and come back to it when you're fresh?" she suggested. "What about a walk round the garden? If it's a plant you're looking for you'll likely find it in the garden."

"A very sensible suggestion," agreed the Reverend.

"And that reminds me—who is going to mow the lawns this summer?"

"What's the matter with Joe Huggs?" asked Mary. Joe Huggs, their handy man, had been laid off during winter, but he always came back in Spring when the garden wanted more seeing to.

"He isn't coming back," said the Reverend. "He finds the extra work too much for him."

"That means the new people up the road have offered him more money. Wait till I get hold of him —I'll give him a piece of my mind."

"I expect he'll keep out of your way," said the

Reverend, mildly. "I'm sure I should if I were in his shoes."

Merriford Vicarage was a great barn of a place; cold, damp and difficult to run, with gardens out of all keeping with present conditions.

Endless stone passages stretched away into a forgotten world of dairies, larders, sculleries, cheese rooms, cellars, attics and outhouses. There were, of course, the network of servants' quarters suitable to a more spacious age.

The Vicar of Merriford was no pauper. It wasn't entirely lack of money that had turned his old home into a domestic nightmare. Since the death of his wife, a dwindling procession of lady-helps, working housekeepers, cook-generals, and daily women had come and gone. Some hadn't stopped to unpack and one had returned in the same cab that had brought her from the station, seven miles away. Even a reformed character, contributed by a home for bad girls, stuck it out for a week and then reckoned there was something to be said for prison after all!

Then came Mary, the bit of flotsam washed up by the fury of the London blitz. During the early days of the war a party of small evacuees had arrived in Merriford, carefully labelled and invoiced, to be distributed among the cottagers. They had been placed on chairs around the little schoolroom to be chosen by kindly foster mothers, one for his blue eyes, another for her brown curls. When the blue eyes and brown curls had been collected and carried away, all the little strangers had been accounted for but one. . . .

Her name was Mary, but that seemed to be all she knew about herself. Her family had disappeared in the blitz, leaving no trace. There she sat, looking solemnly at this strange new world—too young to wonder and much too tired to care.

Mary had found a poor sort of home with old Mrs. Dobbin and, as nobody came to claim her, she passed quietly into the background of village life; until the death of that rather unsatisfactory old-age pensioner left her free to adopt the Vicar of Merriford, and to become something of a foster mother in her own right.

Mary didn't mind scrubbing the stone floors, lighting the fires, doing out the rooms once a week, making the beds, cooking the meals and similar little odd jobs about the house, but she was beginning to find the Reverend a bit of a handful.

Some cold morning when she went upstairs to tidy his bedroom, there would be his woolen under-vest lying on the floor, and it would take her all her time to persuade him to dress all over again.

She liked to get the weekly wash started first thing

on Monday morning but so surely as she got the back kitchen fire going, so surely would she have to run across the fields to the church for the surplice he had left in the vestry.

And what with choosing the hymns for choir practice or remembering how many Sundays it was after Trinity, she had her hands full.

3

MERRIFORD LIES right at the top of the Thames. Geography books will tell you that the Thames is navigable as far as Lechlade, but you don't have to believe everything you read in books.

Now and again, some bold spirit, hiring a boat at the old wharf under the Ha'penny Pike Bridge, will push off into the unknown—feeling, for all the world, like Dr. Livingston and Christopher Columbus rolled into one.

Leaving the Round House on his right, he will

follow the twists and turns of the little river until the great tower of Kempsford church appears across the fields. By pulling his light craft over gravelly shallows he may manage to reach Castle Eaton, or Cricklade, or even Ashton Keynes, but by this time the Thames is little better than a fair-sized brook.

Dragging his boat into the rushes, the explorer will plunge into a meadow of mowing grass and moon daisies, until he arrives at last at Merriford, its church oddly placed in the middle of a field half a mile away from the village.

Very little has changed in Merriford during the last four hundred years. Each winter the meadows are flooded and so have never seen the plough. Great ditches run on both sides of every road, until the stray motorist, suffering from a kind of vertigo, feels himself to be a performer on some precarious tight-rope.

Twice a day, great herds of milking cows, moving thoughtfully from pasture to farmstead and back again, hold up all road traffic. The motorist, caught between deep ditches and the tail of the herd, reflects on the frustration of an invading force faced by such an obstacle. Every movement of his driving wheel is anticipated by the rump of some cud-chewing Friesian. The boy in charge of the herd whistles a sad, lugubrious lullaby, heard on radio the night before last. The day ebbs softly to its close.

Water, water everywhere. Even the boundary line between neighboring counties follows the meandering course of the little shire brook, which has no more sense of direction than a puppy chasing its tail.

In winter, perhaps, a little damp and a little depressing, but with the spring, the boundary brook becomes a blaze of marsh marigolds, the wild iris flaunts its yellow flags along the ditches and we begin to see what God is about when, every year, He sends His flood-waters across Merriford meadows.

The pageant of our summer does not confine itself to the brooks and ditches. Because our wet meadows have never been ploughed they have never lost those wild flowers extinct in more cultivated areas. We can still pick the pasque flower, and a field of autumn crocus is not so strange a sight. The school-mistress at Castle Eaton spent a day in June collecting a hundred and twenty-seven varieties for a wild-flower competition!

Merriford Vicarage was not, in early days, the white elephant it has since become. The new Vicar's young wife was charmed with the large rooms and cool stone passages. She noted with satisfaction that accommodation for the household staff was adequate

—a nice airy room for the two maids and a comfortable sitting-room for the cook-housekeeper.

How fortunate, too, that large lawns ran down to the river—so handy for parish gatherings; while as for the kitchen-gardens, really one could feed the entire village if it came to a pinch. Young Mrs. Stanton had been accustomed to big establishments and with all the village to draw upon for domestic help, a few sculleries and stone passages held no terrors for her. Mowing the lawns would keep the gardener's boy out of mischief.

It was the river at the bottom of the garden that caught her husband's eye. The Thames may not be much of a trout stream, but the angler of catholic tastes can have a lot of fun with the roach, perch and pike along its upper reaches. The new Vicar was no purist. As a boy, he had tried "to plumb the incalculable wonder beneath the water's surface with a stick, a string and a bent pin"; in later life he was a keen fisherman and when, in old age, the angler merged quietly into the naturalist, the little river at the bottom of the Vicarage garden became a never-failing solace and support.

Merriford itself lived up to these favourable first impressions. In those early days, it was a well-ordered little community in which every member played an essential part. Church-going, on Sunday morning, was a pleasant occasion which everybody enjoyed. The girls wore their best frocks and the young fellows went to church to look at their best girls. The old Squire sat in the front pew, turning round to glare at any small boys who might be shuffling their feet behind him. After the service the entire congregation hung round the church gates in little groups, discussing village politics, the drought, or any of those tremendous trifles that might come into their heads.

Faint echoes of old feudal customs still lingered. Much of the land around Merriford was owned by an Oxford college and, on audit day, each tenant farmer was still handed a pair of white gloves—worn in church on the following Sunday, to let his neighbors know that his rent had been well and truly paid. A trifle of history which proves the admirable liaison existing between church and landlord as lately as the close of the last century.

Family prayers were not unknown. A young man, visiting relations, found the household on their knees and crept into an empty place, which happened to be among the maids. His uncle began a prayer: "Almighty God, in whose sight all men are equal—Jack, you're sitting among the servants—grant we beseech Thee—"

From which it will be gathered that the young Vicar of Merriford entered on his new job under the happiest auspices. The Golden Age was passing; wars and national disasters were to scatter cherished beliefs like chaff, but the time was not yet. God was very much in His Heaven and all was well with His world.

4

CLOSE ON fifty years had slipped quietly by since the Reverend first came to Merriford.

It hadn't, of course, been roses all the way. There was that dreadful poisoning case, when he had found three dead trout floating in the Thames at the bottom of his garden, and he had written to the *Field* about it.

The letter was published, with a rather strong note by the Editor on the subject of river pollution, and several readers sent their suggestions as to the cause of the trouble. One keen fisherman was sufficiently interested to come all the way down to Merriford to probe the matter a little further.

He found the Vicar running a light mower between the graves, and the two of them passed into the church, where the stranger admired the interesting old woodwork, the Norman arch, and the Jacobean pulpit. He agreed with the Vicar that the restoration work carried out in the late seventies had some regrettable features, but gave it as his considered opinion that the building, taking it all in all, ranked among the most interesting on that countryside. Then he got down to the sad story of the dead trout. . . .

The Vicar was delighted to exchange ideas with a brother angler—and a little flattered that his letter had roused such interest. So they sat together in the south aisle, just under the seventeenth-century window, and probed the mystery from every possible point of view.

After lunch at the Vicarage, they took a walk along the river, had a chat with the farmer through whose fields it ran; took a sample of the water, and checked up any possible sources of pollution on a large-scale ordnance map. Altogether, he spent a most enjoyable afternoon with a highly intelligent companion.

The Reverend was a real countryman; all his interests were concerned with country things—but it was refreshing to have an occasional chat with some-one who spoke one's own language. The stranger's interest in the church, for instance! He hadn't wandered round, talking a lot of half-baked plati-tudes; his appreciation of the font and the Early Eng-lish arch had been quite scholarly, and when it came to fishing he really did know what he was talking about. . . .

A week later, Mr. Hyatt, the farmer, stormed into the Vicarage garden. He had that morning received a letter from the Thames Conservancy suggesting that the effluvium—whatever *that* was—from his new cheese-making machine was polluting the river and killing all the fish. What the hell did the Vicar mean by snooping round with one of their inspectors?

The poor Vicar was bewildered. Hyatt was, as a rule, such a fair-minded man. He attempted to pour the oil of reason upon these troubled waters.

"Really, Mr. Hyatt," he began, "there's no need to be violent . . ."

"Violent!" snorted the incensed farmer. "Wouldn't *you* be violent if someone wrote a lot of lies about you and then came crawling into your place, trying to prove that his lies were true."

"Really, Hyatt," said the Vicar, "I haven't the

slightest idea what you're talking about. You must be mad."

"I'm mad all right," agreed Mr. Hyatt. "I'd like to chuck you and your inspector into the river and see how long it would take for my—my *effluvium* to poison the pair of you."

"No need to be violent," repeated the Vicar. "And who is this inspector you keep on talking about?"

"You should know," said Mr. Hyatt, darkly. "I saw the two of you prowling along the river—why, you came into my yard and stood talking to me for the best part of ten minutes."

The Vicar began to see daylight. "Oh, *that* fellow," he smiled.

"Yes, *that* fellow," echoed Mr. Hyatt.

"No more an inspector than you are," laughed the Vicar. "Just an ordinary visitor who had a look round the church and took a little walk along the river."

"He may be all you say," grunted the farmer, "but he took a sample of water where my swill brook joins the river and sent a report to the Thames Conservancy that will cost me the thick end of a hundred pounds before I'm through with it."

"What do you want me to do?" asked the Vicar.

"Nothing!" replied Mr. Hyatt. "You've done a heck of a sight too much already!"—and he stumped out of the study.

That bit of trouble had blown over. Mr. Hyatt was a good old sort and bore no malice—especially as poisoning the baby Thames did not cost him "the thick end of a hundred pounds," as he feared. But the Reverend was more careful in the future and viewed plausible strangers, who admired his Jacobean pulpit, with a slightly jaundiced eye.

He was more fortunate in his encounter with Mrs. Gossop, a real, old busybody, who lived in that long, low house facing the Green. Mrs. Gossop was always putting everybody to rights. Before she had been in the village two minutes, she started "creating" about the housing shortage and called a meeting at the school to go into the question. One or two villagers went along to hear what she had to say. She turned up with a great pile of papers, and her main point was that no new house had been built in Merriford for the last fifty years. There was a lot of talk about tied cottages, appalling living conditions, insanitary wells and so on, until her audience began to wonder how any of them had managed to keep alive all those years. Mrs. Gossop was so sorry for them that they almost began to be sorry for themselves.

Finally, after reading a lot of bylaws and reports from the Ministry, she banged on her great pile of papers, called them all a lot of down-trodden serfs and asked the Reverend, who was in the chair, what he was going to do about it.

"Pardon me," said the Reverend, "wouldn't it be fairer to ask what *you* are going to do about it?"

Mrs. G. was a bit flabbergasted at this. "Me!" she snapped. "What has your housing shortage to do with me?"

The old Reverend looked over his spectacles. "Mrs. Gossop doesn't seem to realize," he said quietly, "that she is at present occupying three cottages which were converted into one dwelling house shortly before she came to the village. Of course it would ease the shortage if. . . ."

Mrs. Gossop lost all interest in the housing problem and started another hare. "Even more important than cottages," she said, "is the waste paper problem. So far as I can gather no arrangements have been made for the collection of waste paper. The collection of waste paper should be undertaken by some responsible person working in touch with the Rural District Council. . . ."

The Reverend looked at Mrs. Gossop and her great pile of papers, and said: "I entirely agree. The collection of any available waste paper is a vital link in our modern economy. I propose, from the chair, that Mrs. Gossop be invited to undertake this important task. She has, already, made quite a good start!"

Mrs. Gossop never forgave him for that. Ever after, she was always trying to put a spoke in his wheel. But it was a long time before she called any more meetings.

Then, much later, after Mary had come to the Vicarage, there was the famous Battle of the Mushroom Field.

In every parish there is always one field of old pasture where mushrooms grow. You don't have to do anything about them—they just grow!

There was a wonderful mushroom field at Merriford. Every autumn, if the summer hadn't been too dry, it was covered with little white buttons, which appeared during the night and had all gone before breakfast.

The law, as it relates to mushrooms, has always been a little obscure. Farmers aren't too pleased to see people wandering over their fields, but the season is short and very few strangers are about so early in the morning. The villagers, accustomed to enjoying the fruits of the earth in their season, pick the mushrooms as a matter of course. If their right to do so is challenged, you can look out for trouble.

Mr. Hyatt, a reasonable man who only shouted at you under the stress of extreme provocation, didn't mind how many of his neighbors enjoyed his mushrooms. So long as they caused him no trouble—as the parson had done when he found a few dead trout in the river—he couldn't see that much harm was done. Let them have their mushrooms—so long as they didn't ask him to eat the wretched things!

When Mr. Hyatt died and his farm was sold, the new man clamped down on the mushroom field as if it had been a shop window full of precious jewels. He locked the gates, wired the weak places in the hedges, and put up notices to say that trespassers would be prosecuted with the utmost vigour of the law. The villagers only laughed at him and went on picking his mushrooms the same as before.

Then he caught one of his own men red-handed. He called in the police, and, before you could look round, there was a case before the Magistrates, with the Vicar subpoenaed to give evidence.

The Reverend was in a bit of a cleft stick. Both sides wanted him to speak for them and he wasn't easy in his own mind as to which of them was in the right. Quite probably, the owner of the field had the law on his side, but during all the years he had been in charge of the parish, it had never occurred to him that anyone could possibly object. The former owner, Mr. Hyatt, had been very reasonable about it. Really, the whole affair was most regrettable . . . so bad for the village . . . after all a few mushrooms more or less. . . .

The prosecuting solicitor wasn't getting much change out of his witness so he tried to see what a little sarcasm would do.

"You aren't, by any chance, allergic to mushrooms?" he inquired smoothly.

"Oh dear, no," smiled the Vicar.

"You don't happen to be one of those prejudiced people who won't eat them on principle?"

The Reverend replied that so far from being prejudiced he often enjoyed a mushroom with his fried bacon.

"What time does the man call?" asked the young solicitor.

"Which man?" blinked the Reverend over his spectacles.

"The man with the mushrooms!" snapped the lawyer.

"I'm sure I couldn't say," replied the Reverend. To do him justice the point had never occurred to him. "I'm afraid you would have to ask Mary. She interviews all the tradesmen. Yes, Mary would know."

"Very well," said the prosecuting solicitor, "we'll ask Mary."

So Mary Dobbin was called into the witness box,

and the same question was repeated. On what day did the man call with the mushrooms?

"There's no man," said Mary.

"Really! Do you grow the mushrooms—in one of the cellars?"

"No," said Mary. "I go out very early in the morning and pick them."

"In what we have heard described as the Mushroom Field?"

"Of course!" said Mary.

"You say you get up very early in the morning. Why?"

"To be there before all the others start picking them."

"Does it occur to you, Miss—Miss Dobbin, that you are trespassing?"

"What—in the Mushroom Field?" asked Mary.

"Of course! After all, the field does belong to my client. He bought it and paid for it. Surely he has a right to his own mushrooms?"

"As much right as the rest of us," said Mary. "Anyone can pick mushrooms. Nobody planted them so they belong to everybody—the same as sticklebacks in the Sherry,* or blackberries, or snakesheads in the North Meadow."

* Shire Brook.

"That is how *you* feel about it," sniffed the solicitor.

"That's how anybody feels about it, if they've got any sense," said Mary.

"But suppose somebody came into your employer's garden and picked any flowers they fancied?"

"They do," said Mary. "They get into our shrubbery and punish the aconites, something cruel."

"And how does your employer like that?"

"He doesn't mind," said Mary. "There's enough for all of us—same as the mushrooms."

"You still don't get my point," complained the lawyer, as one dealing with a rather backward child. "There is still the question of damage. When you go tramping down all my client's valuable mowing grass. . . ."

"No fear of that," said Mary. "I'm in my bare feet."

"So you're in your bare feet. Now why is that, I wonder?"

"I don't want to get my best shoes wet," explained Mary.

"Your best shoes! Why your best shoes?"

"Because it's Sunday."

"Ah, so you only go trespassing on Sunday. The better the day, the better the misdeed. Now tell the Court why, when you feel like stealing my client's property, you always select the Sabbath."

"Because, for one thing," explained Mary, "folk lie in bed longer on Sunday and I don't have to be about so early to get ahead of them."

"Very ingenious! And what is your other excuse?"

"I like the Reverend to have a good, solid breakfast on Sunday, because he's got such a long day in front of him. So I give him a nice plateful of bacon and mushrooms."

"I see! You don't like a nice plate of mushrooms yourself, of course!"

"No," said Mary. "I never eat mushrooms—they bring me out in spots."

5

THE REVEREND would have found it difficult to say when the bottom fell out of his little world.

There were the two wars, of course, each marked with a personal disaster—his only son, John, fresh from his College O.T.C., killed in 1918, a few days before the Armistice; and his wife, Margaret, victim of the second war, when a bomb fell on the Guards Chapel during a memorial service—but what family had not been so stricken? The Reverend was not one to turn his face to the wall. Having written "Thy Will Be Done" on the little memorial brass under the west window of his parish church, he had returned to the ruins of his family life, and, in the pact he had made with his God, he had found peace.

The village seemed to have suffered most, though you couldn't put your hand on any particular change for the worse. Something had gone and nothing new had come to take its place. The village boys didn't touch their caps any more. No harm in that, but now, when they met you, they didn't seem to know what to do with their hands. They had lost their taste for leadership but they missed their old leaders. Perhaps they even missed the discipline of those old days when the Parson was really somebody, and the old Squire was a power in the land.

One thing was certain: they weren't going to have any more of *that*. They weren't quite sure what *that* was, but they weren't going to have any more of it— an attitude of mind that left them a little suspicious, a little unsure of themselves and a little unhappy.

The trouble was that when *that* went so many nice things went with it. The cricket club hadn't started again. The social club hadn't started again. The flower show hadn't started again. What was everybody's business was nobody's business.

All the young fellows wanted to play cricket but none of them wanted to do the work. They missed their social club, but no one would take on the job of secretary. Everybody talked about the wonderful old flower show, but nobody had the guts to gamble with the weather on a particular English Saturday.

Without knowing it, Merriford had reached the end of an era—two world wars had flattened out the traditional features of rural England. In the old days, before the first war, the little community was nicely graded and worked like a well-oiled machine. Looking back, you might ask by what right a certain individual had done certain things; by what right a certain man took the seat at the top of the table; by what right one woman gave away the prizes while another washed up the cups and saucers at the back of the tea tent.

Hard questions to answer, and asking them was a waste of time. The old way of life, for what it was worth, had gone. The cricket club had gone; the social club had gone; the flower show had gone; even *that* had gone—and no one seemed any the happier for its going.

The Reverend, pondering these present discontents, was hard put to it to reach any conclusion satisfying to a fair-minded man. He had no politics, but he knew that all this talk about one man being as good as another was, at best, a long-term plan—like running a cricket team. You provided the nets, but only the boys who took the trouble to practice got into the team. The others lay around on the grass and groused because they weren't playing.

It wasn't fair to say that the people who ran the show before the wars were hanging back to prove that the new order wouldn't work. Either they had been taxed out of existence, or they were to old, or they were dead. The old Squire had gone; the manor had been turned into a girls' school, and of those boys who played cricket on the "purley" only a few old men were left. The others—the best—having fought their good fight had heard the sound of the trumpets and—with John and Margaret—had passed safely over to the other side.

Of course, things would right themselves in time. Some young parson would come along and get them going, as he had done fifty years ago. Yes, some young fellow. At this point in his ruminations the old man always felt a slight tightening at the heart. Was that what was wrong with Merriford? Was he getting too old for his work? Would a younger man do a better job? The old, familiar doubts darted and dived at him like angry bees: "Too old, too old, too old—get out and make room for a better man."

But was he too old? Surely, being Vicar of a country parish was an old man's job. The country, itself, was too old and set in its habits to cope with a young incumbent. All it asked was to drift along, singing the old hymns to the old tunes, believing the old beliefs. The country had no use for earnest young curates, cheerful young curates or any kind of curate, if it came to that. Being preached at by one of these young fellows was like being shaved by a lather-boy. What did they know about life and death, or what to say to some poor soul when the shadow of the dark angel fell across the lintel of a cottage door?

So the Reverend tried to argue himself out of his black mood; whistling his courage up, but with no particular result. For he did not need reminding that although he had become Vicar of a country parish while still in his twenties, he hadn't made such a bad job of it.

Meanwhile, congregations were dwindling and it seemed that he would soon have the church to himself. What would one of those young fellows do about that, he wondered. You couldn't stampede a village into holiness. John Wesley had done it, but he was no Wesley. Perhaps one of those young fellows. . . .

In his early days, the Reverend had wasted a lot of good time preparing a lot of poor sermons but, later on, he was apt to let his notes fall to the floor of the pulpit and talk to his listeners as man to man.

One Sunday morning he addressed a rather sparse congregation on the advantages of Sunday Observance. "Last night," he said, "I had a rather curious dream. I dreamt that one of my parishioners, who is at present checking his football pool, arrived at the gates of heaven and was surprised to find that no adequate arrangements had been made for his reception.

"He complained to the custodian who replied, rather fairly, I thought: 'My dear fellow, how can you expect me to recognize you when I haven't seen you in church since you were christened—forty-five years ago?' "

From which it will be gathered that the Reverend was becoming a bit of a character; one of those rare, ripe, robust country parsons who care deeply for their fellows, and have too much respect for the Almighty to meddle largely in His affairs. Men like Hawker of of Morwenstow, who wrote the Song of the Western Men; Parson Jack Russell, whose memorial is the happy little terrier that bears his name; or, more lately, Parson Jack Gibbs who hunted five days a week in the Duke's country, and, within living memory, announced the Meets of Hounds from his pulpit —such are the salt of our good English earth.

The Reverend came of this sound stock. He would not have been greatly concerned with dogma even if he had known what it was all about. He loved every man and woman in Merriford; he hoped he was on the right road to Heaven, and the more people he could persuade to join him the better he was pleased.

AND THEN the Americans came to Merriford. The uneasy peace, following the second World War, was just five years old when Reuben Watts burst into the taproom of the Thatchers Arms with a strange tale to tell.

"War hev started all over agen," he announced. "They Americans has landed and has took the old Airdrome."

A fellow ancient spat solemnly into the sawdust.

"Who stuffed 'ee up wi' all that old rubbish?" he asked.

" 'Taint rubbish," retorted old Reuben. "I see'd the thing wi' my own eyes, I tell 'ee. 'Undreds of 'em, scurrying about like a lot uv emmets. Comical young chaps in such colored shirts and weskits as you never did behold."

Investigation proved that old Reuben was very nearly right. A detachment of American engineers had indeed taken over the derelict landing ground, abandoned after the war, and were converting it into an advanced Air Base to protect the Free World from Russian and Mongol hordes.

Modern international politics are a bit confusing at the best of times and it was not surprising that old Reuben, wandering over the former airfield in search of plovers' eggs, had arrived at the only possible conclusion: another war had started. The Americans were invading England and their advanced troops had already taken the old airdrome.

It took some of the best brains available at the Thatchers Arms to work out the political implications of an American Air Base in the British Isles. But the thing had certainly happened, and new wonders proceeded to descend upon Merriford on each succeeding day.

First came the giant bulldozers, followed by fearful mechanical contrivances which dug valleys and dropped hills into them. Whole farms were laid as flat as the fens. Nothing was sacred. The avenue of fine elms leading to the ancient gatehouse of a local mansion was torn up and the owner fled in panic from the accursed place.

Public highways were diverted. The road from Merriford to Little Summerford was closed down, to the utter consternation of old Mrs. Poole who had a married daughter living in the neighboring hamlet. The Americans, after consultation with Washington and two public inquiries, built another and finer road round the outer perimeter of the Air Base, but local landowners were furious at such poaching on their preserves. The friendly invaders, full of good intentions, were baffled to find themselves building up a heavy debit of ill-will.

Failing to please anybody, they settled down to the job of constructing a three-mile runway with a gusto that seemed positively indecent to the simple villagers, who saw their dearest possessions being swept away before their eyes. First to go was the mushroom field, followed by the fritillary meadow and the peewit ground, while the tall elms fell like ninepins at a fair.

Lesser landmarks: the hollow tree where the rock pigeons built, the rookery in Long Meadow, and

Clematis Lane, patronized by courting couples for the past hundred years, disappeared in a night and with them went the old double bank, home of elder-berries and wild sloes from which the cottagers had brewed the potent drinks which made glad the heart of man at Christmastide.

All these things could have been forgiven, but the passing of Snowstorm Cover was the last, the final straw that broke the patient camel's back.

Once again old Reuben was the harbinger of ill-tidings. On a Saturday morning when hounds were due to meet at Merriford cross-roads, he left his cot-tage at the crack of dawn to walk over to Snowstorm and stop the big earth before the old fox had re-turned from its nightly prowl.

As he trundled his way through the wet dew, heavily loaded with mattock and spade, old Reuben saw his immediate future stretching out before him as in a vision. The hounds would draw the kale in Seventeen Acres and, having found, the old varmint would lead them a merry dance before heading back for the sanctuary of his earth in the lew of Snowstorm Cover. To find, of course, that old Reuben had been there afore him and that his earth had been well and truly stopped.

After the kill the Master would want to know what splendid fellow had stopped the earth, and

Reuben, happening along at the right moment, would be handed the half-crown on which so much Saturday night happiness would depend.

Such were his happy daydreams, as the old man plodded through the wet grass; the rising sun glinting on the diamond-studded cobwebs, hanging like fairy filigree across his path!

But where *was* Snowstorm Cover? Reuben rubbed his eyes, spat, and rubbed his eyes again. Snowstorm Cover had disappeared, vanished, and where it had been was a shambles of broken tree-trunks lying about in drunken disarray. The Americans had been there before him and Snowstorm Cover, after the passing of the bulldozers, the scoops and the mechanical shovels, was as though it had never been.

Back to the village hurried old Reuben with yet another tale to tell. If these Americans could do away with a fox-cover they could do away with anything. No one was safe. What was the village policeman doing? Nice thing, indeed, when a pack of foreigners could come along and steal a fox-cover without so much as a by-your-leave!

He would go and see the Reverend. That was the plan. The Reverend always knew what was best to be done. Old Reuben hurried off to set in motion the machinery that would bring retribution to these guilty men.

But what was that? From far across the fields, borne on the clear, crisp air of an autumn morning, came the sound of the huntsman's horn.

Like an old war horse stirred by the sound of a distant bugle, old Reuben was up and away; across the park, right-handed along the brook, caught up in that dratted barbed wire.

For hounds had found in the kale, the old varmint was on the move—and yet another international crisis had been happily averted.

The engineers, having done their damndest, departed and the little American town they had built on the far corner of the Air Base was occupied by a very different type of invader. Those pick-and-shovel boys had been rather rough diamonds, up to any sort of mischief, from starting a little war on their own to poaching the trout in preserved waters. But the technical types who followed them were a less alarming breed.

Of course they continued to drive on the wrong side of the road, as is the habit of all foreigners when visiting these islands. They collected on bridges and in the bar parlors of ancient inns, like swallows getting ready to fly south and their talk was all of strange, exotic things from home runs to honey buckets. At regular intervals, they were smitten by a fearful homesickness for one-street towns of white, wooden houses, a drug store and the hot Texas sun shining down over all. They produced, on the slightest provocation, well-thumbed pictures of "back home" and they behaved, in fact, like any body of reasonable young men who find themselves fed-up, a little bewildered and far from home.

The worst that could be said of them was that they started all the village maidens chewing gum with the exception of Mrs. Gossop, who had long ago put away from her all evil things, and Mary at the Vicarage who had no time for that sort of nonsense.

These Americans had a nice sense of dead-pan humor; as when old Reuben caught a working party fixing a red homing light to the spire of Merriford parish church. Having contemplated the strange scene for the better part of a morning he questioned a junior electrician as to the reasons for this sacrilegious act.

The young American, with a wink at his companions, explained that the church was in a direct line with the runway and that the spire, being a danger to machines coming in to land at the Air Base, would have to be pulled down.

"But you can't do that," said Reuben. "I do remember when they ran a steeplechase round the old spire and back again. You just wait till I tells the Reverend—he'll be on your track smartish."

"We didn't come to your blooming country to break our necks," the young fellow reminded him. "And when did *you* go to church last?"

"A man's religion," said Reuben, "is a man's own business."

"Drinking's your business, and, talking of drink— we're moving the pub tomorrow."

"*Moving the pub!*" gasped old Reuben. "And where to might you be moving the pub?"

"Over to Marston," replied the boy, with another wink at his buddies.

"*Over to Marston,*" repeated the astonished veteran. "But they've got a pub at Marston a'ready, so they have. And what's going to happen to we at Merriford when you've moved the pub over to Marston?"

"You'll have to walk over to Marston. Work up a nice thirst so you will," replied the American, dropping into the local vernacular.

"My thirst never wants no working up," old Reuben told him, "and if you thinks I be going to traipse across all they fields every time I wants to wet my whistle, you be wrong, mister."

"Take your choice," said the American. "It's the

church or the pub. You can't have them both. Which is it to be?"

"We'll keep the pub," said Reuben, firmly. "But dont'ee go telling the Reverend as I bargained with 'ee. The Reverend do set unaccountable great store by the old church, so he do."

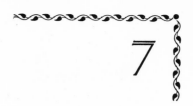

7

MONTHS SLIPPED BY; the Air Base was completed, and the jets flew in non-stop from Texas. Great silver monsters, shining in the moonlight, roared over the roof-tops and Merriford was frightened out of its five wits.

Nothing heard or seen during the two wars could compare with it. The noise was continuous. No sooner had one machine flattened out to land on the new three-mile runway than another was circling round to take its place in the queue.

The next morning the village was in an uproar, and the Thatchers Arms was buzzing like an angry hive. What were these Americans doing in Merriford? Why couldn't they stop in their own country and leave decent folk in peace? Dark tales were told of underground galleries packed with hydrogen bombs which might blow up at any moment. Rabbits, driven in from the surrounding countryside, were eating all the young cabbages in all the allotments. Game preserves were being ruined. The value of property had dropped by half. . . .

Great gravel pits yawned where fertile farms had been. Lorries and staff cars swept down country lanes —always on the wrong side of the roads. Death and danger lurked round every corner.

The most frightening thing of all was the noise. All flying, it seemed, had to be done at night. During the day-time the great 'silver bellies' sat quietly behind their barbed wire, but, come evening, the three-mile runway sprang to light and life; engines roared and the earth shook. Peace gave way to pandemonium.

So that, what with the noise, the lack of sleep and the rabbits, relations between young America and old England became a trifle strained.

Sensing that all was not well, a slightly worried Base Commander paid a semi-official visit to the

Vicarage. The Reverend sat in his study and listened to the sad story of a great and friendly nation misunderstood by the very people it was trying to save. It might, his visitor admitted, be an exaggeration to liken Merriford to a dog biting the hand that fed it, but she certainly resembled a sinking ship turning all her guns on her would-be rescuers.

"Perhaps they don't want to be rescued," suggested the Reverend. "They may not even know that they are sinking. By the way, *are* we sinking?"

The Base Commander set about convincing this odd old man that, financially, Britain was on her beam-ends. "Otherwise," he asked, "why should my country have to pour money into Europe and organize your defences on such a colossal scale?"

The Reverend was no politician and the situation was a little beyond him. International altruism is a rare bird and not easily recognized, but this young fellow seemed very sure of his ground. Perhaps Merriford had been a little lacking in the courtesies. "Tell me, my boy," he said, "what have my people been doing to hurt your feelings?"

"They don't like us," was the reply. "They treat us like a lot of interlopers, and it hurts—yes, sir!"

"Very discouraging," murmured the Reverend. "Friendship enforced can be a very delicate plant. You had similar trouble, I gather, when you first occupied your own great country. The natives were frequently unwilling, were they not, to give up their lands and complained that you destroyed their hunting grounds? So they scalped you!"

The American rose stiffly. "I won't waste your time further," he said. "I didn't come here to be laughed at."

"My dear fellow," said the old man, "I'm not laughing. I'm trying to help. Don't you realize that what happened then is happening again today? With the very best intentions you are taking over our farms and destroying our hunting grounds. Some of us have even been driven from our homes. You have replaced these happy scenes with a three-mile runway and you have made our nights hideous with your infernal machines. No doubt we should be grateful; no doubt we shall be grateful, but you must give us time. Just at the moment we are feeling like your poor benighted Indians who didn't know what was good for them. You get my point?"

"Sure," said the Base Commander, "sure, I get your point, and you've driven it well home, but you can't blame my boys. They're sick as hell with the whole business. All they ask is to be back home where they rightly belong; and when they get nothing but ugly looks, it hurts. You get *my* point, I guess?"

"What do you want me to do?" asked the Reverend.

"Next time you're in your pulpit, padre, why not tell your folk the facts of life. If you're shy, I'll send my chaplain along—"

"And the two of us could make a duet of it?" This picture of two preachers in one pulpit, telling Britain that she was now a poor relation, was too much for the Reverend's sense of humor. "I'm afraid that isn't the answer," he smiled.

"Then what do we do?" asked the Colonel. "Sit around and wait for the blowup? Suppose your boys, or my boys, start something."

8

THAT "SOMETHING" started sooner than anyone expected. July the Fourth, a date not unconnected with American history, opened with a light spatter of rain giving promise of a warm, cloudless day. The haymakers were about early and by ten o'clock the sun blazed from a clear sky. Bees were busy among the lime blossoms; children picnicked in a corner of the hayfield, gathering bunches of moon daisies and meadowsweet; pink dog-roses clambered riotously over the hedges. . . .

Strong men labored in the fields, one thought uppermost in their minds. Come evening, they would seek the cool, beer-scented taproom of the Thatchers Arms, where the mighty hogshead of midsummer cider was already in position. And what animal juices had been stolen by the hot sunshine would be returned a thousandfold.

To the average townsman, cider is a weak, anaemic, non-alcoholic beverage, fit only for babes and sucklings. It is sold in milk-bars and similar non-licensed premises under a variety of deceptive labels. Such wish-wash may be cider of sorts but it is not the cider brewed for haymakers in the villages of the Vale.

Tapping the big sixty-gallon cask at the Thatchers Arms is an annual event, a tradition and a solemn rite. A *vendange* in the vineyards of France is a pale shadow of the real thing as we know it in Merriford. Quite ridiculous, it is for chance visitors to the Côte d'Or to return with travellers' tales of wine-tasting in cellars filled from the original wine press of the Dukes of Burgundy. Useless also is it to remind us how Colonel Brisson halted his regiment and ordered them to present arms when passing Clos Vougeot; or to relate how Abbot Jean de Bussières gave thirty barrels of that delectable wine to Pope Gregory XI and was made a Cardinal for his courtesy. Such trivial legends cut no ice at the Thatchers Arms when the big cider cask is poised for tapping.

A pleasant feature of this ceremonial cider tasting is that no man is expected to deliver judgment on the vintage until he has drained his quart pot and placed it bottom-up on the counter. No rolling a thimbleful round your palate and spitting it on the floor at the Thatchers Arms. You drain your first quart as a sampler and a second quart—just to make sure. Then you settle down to the serious business of drinking. But don't forget that cider, real cider, is potent stuff— particularly after the fourth pint, when it operates suddenly, like the kick of a mule. If you are wise, you will arrange in advance for your nearest neighbor to support you on the journey home; and, even then, with the blind leading the blind, both have been known to fall into the ditch.

At the Thatchers Arms the stage was set. There stood the great cider cask flanked by mighty flagons, lesser pewter tankards and those puny pint pots for the less adventurous. Along the bar were draped all those thirsty souls who, having endured the burden and heat of the day, were now worthy of their reward.

Zero hour had struck—when, down the lane, heralded by sounds of revelry, came a party of ten American airmen who seemed to have been celebrating something up at the Air Base. Borne on the wings of syncopated melody, they flowed into the bar and clamored for more of the strange drinks on which they had already laid the firm foundations of an evening's merriment.

The fat landlord, with a solemn wink at his particular cronies, filled ten of his mightiest flagons from the great cask and deployed them in single file before his expectant guests.

"On the house, gentlemen!" he announced.

The young Americans gazed in astonishment at this formidable array; until one, finding his voice at last, inquired what this strange concoction might be.

"Cider," said the fat landlord. Upon which, a three-months enlisted airman of the 3rd class told a fully-licensed landlord what he thought of cider in general, of this cider in particular; and, furthermore, what the landlord could do with his cider. "Take it away," said the airman, "and bring me a man's drink."

"Cider," the fat landlord told him, "be a man's drink, but I doubts whether you be man enough to drink it. No, nor your young friends neither!"

Such was the challenge, such the gage. The haymakers looked curiously at the Americans and the Americans looked, not without apprehension, at the ten massive tankards. But there could be no going back. Honor lost—all lost. Stiffly, as at a ceremonial drill, ten young airmen grasped the handles of ten quart pots—all together boys, down the hatch—and plunged bravely into the unknown!

Not Washington at Yorktown, nor Nelson at Trafalgar struck a shrewder blow for national honor than did those ten unknown warriors at the Thatchers Arms. And had they known when to stop all might have been well.

But young America lacked that discretion which is the better part of valor. Like Prince Rupert at Naseby, they continued their impetuous pursuit of the beaten enemy long after the battle had been fairly won.

And so lost the day!

As those cavaliers rode stirrup to stirrup in the charge, so young America drank tankard to tankard with those strong men of the Thatchers Arms who had sweated themselves bone-dry from sunrise to sunset. The odds were too heavy; the tankards were too deep; the cider had been too long i' the barrel.

But it was good while it lasted. Good to drink as man to man, to feel the generous fluid seeping down to the very roots of your being. Good to know that a younger civilization could hold its own with a brave, old world. Good to be accepted by these fine British yeomen as every sort of a regular guy. Good to know that you had been weighed in the balance,

with how many reputed pints, and not found want-
ing.

Came closing time. Just one more for the road . . .
the road . . . but where was the road . . . and
whither . . . to whatsoever . . . to whithersoever . . .
roads . . . roads . . . roads. . . .

Rough but kindly hands tried to sort out the tangle
that had once been ten American airmen of the 3rd
class, but so surely as they rescued one inert form
from the shambles, so inevitably did two other airmen claim him as a man and a brother and draw him
back into the quivering heap.

Until at last, old Reuben reckoned the only thing
to be done was to "prop 'em up one agen 'tother,
give 'em a shove-like, and see what 'appens!"

What happened was a serpentine movement across
a field of growing barley, down the bank of the old
canal and into the washpool at Sheepscombe Bottom
—singing, singing all the way!

"I have come," said the American Colonel, "to
apologize for the unpardonable happenings of last
night."

The Reverend blinked at his visitor over the top
of his reading glasses. "Last night!" he repeated. "Did
anything unusual happen last night—beyond a cer-

tain amount of singing which we rather anticipated on Independence Day?"

"Ten of my men," explained the Colonel sombrely, "failed to return to Base. At daybreak, we sent out search parties. One was found asleep in the middle of a field of barley."

"That left nine!" said the Reverend.

"Another was suspended from the barbed wire surrounding the field."

"Eight still unaccounted for!" smiled the Vicar.

"A third," continued the Base Commander, "was trying to save a comrade from drowning in the old canal. Fortunately for them both the canal has no water in it."

"That left six!" chuckled the old man.

"The remainder were lying in a heap in a disused washpool . . ."

"And how are they feeling this morning?" asked the Vicar.

"Still unconscious!"

"All of them?"

"All of them!"

"A great tribute to our local cider," said the Vicar.

"That is what I came to see you about. Is it possible, do you think, that their drinks had been tampered with in any way?"

"Oh dear me, no!" the Reverend assured him.

"Our harvest cider is grand stuff, grand stuff. It has to be when you think of men working in the fields all day. You see, when the weather holds they carry on till dark and they need something stronger than light ale when they knock off at night."

"I always thought cider was a soft drink," said the Colonel.

"That's where your boys were caught napping," explained the Vicar. "I wouldn't be too hard on them. They behaved very well under the circumstances."

That was too much for the Base Commander: "It's lucky you don't have to hold up discipline at an Air Base," he spluttered. "Ten men outside the wire without passes at six o'clock in the morning isn't funny. No, sir!"

"Nine times out of ten you would be right," the Reverend told him, "but this is the odd case. I've had Brooks, the landlord, up to see me. He was worried about his license. My people don't come to church much these days, but you'll always find them at the Vicar's back door when they're in trouble. Brooks tells me that these lads dropped in just as he was broaching the big cider cask and that when he invited them to join the party they jollied him and his customers about grown men and soft drinks. Brooks ex-

plained that cider, as we know it, is a man's drink—
if a man is man enough to drink it."

"That put them on the spot, I guess," laughed the
Colonel. "And did my boys stand up to be counted?"

"They certainly did," replied the Reverend. "So
long as they could stand—they stood up to be
counted."

9

SUMMER HAD elbowed Spring out of the Vicarage garden and only a few wisps of wistaria were left to tell the tale. Just outside the Vicarage back door, Mary had hung a large carpet on the line and was beating the bejabers out of it with a clothes-prop as big as herself.

Tuesday was Mary's day for doing out the drawing-room and she was putting everything she knew into the job . . . But the clothes-prop took a bit of handling.

Round the corner drifted an American airman who leaned against the trunk of an apple tree, smiling at the unequal conflict.

"Say, sister," he laughed, "what has the poor thing done that you should treat it so tough?"

Mary laid off the carpet and turned on the intruder. "Who are you?" she asked. "Another of those Americans?"

"How did you guess?" asked the boy.

"No mistaking your noisy lot," sniffed Mary.

"Noisy!" echoed the American. "She calls us noisy."

"Last Saturday night," said Mary sternly, "you were all terrible. We could hear you creating all the way back to the camp. Shouting and singing."

"Crooning!" corrected the American. "Just a bunch of orphans crooning lullabies to keep them from crying their eyes out. You were never an orphan."

"That's where you're wrong," said Mary. "And orphans don't have to act so daft."

"Celebrating!" said the American. "The boys were celebrating. . . ."

"You're always celebrating something."

"There's always something to celebrate," admitted the American, sadly, "and do we suffer in the morning!"

"Serves you right," said the girl. "Now run along and leave me in peace. I've got work to do."

"I'll be around, tomorrow?"

"Tomorrow," said Mary. "I'll be washing the surplices."

"Okay, see you Thursday then."

"Thursday is choir practice."

"Lady," said the boy, sadly, "you work too hard. I'll have the Union on you. We'll picket this dump."

"You are a one," said Mary, now somewhat amused at his persistence.

"Tell me your name," he said.

"Mary, what's yours."

"Johnny Fedora," replied the American solemnly. "It is a sort of nickname I picked up because my father owns a haberdashery in Dallas. When I come around Friday I'll tell you about it."

"That's the day I do out the Reverend's study," said Mary with a smile.

The fact that a young American finally went away telling the world that it was a beautiful morning had nothing to do, of course, with a young girl, pretty as a picture working her heart out in a parsonage.

For the first time in months Mr. Fedora (better stick to his nickname now we've started that way) felt there might be something to be said for Collective Defence and better Anglo-American relations. Nobody liked the bright lights better than Mr. Fedora, but how could they compare with the soft peace of an English garden . . . pigeons splashing out of tall elms . . . and a girl beating the bejabers out of a carpet with a clothes-prop as big as herself?

"Oh, what a beautiful morning," carolled Mr. Fedora; and "Oh what a beautiful day," whistled a thrush in the Vicarage shrubbery . . . Well, they should know!

The next morning, bright and early, found Johnny walking through the wet grass of the Vicarage orchard, but early as it was, Mary was already on top of a ladder trying to persuade the climbing Lady Hillingdon to stick to her moorings on the south wall of the Vicarage. There had been a bit of a blow during the night and it was difficult to say which part of the landscape was the girl on the ladder and which part a lot of yellow roses waving in the wind.

Mary was so wrapped up in her job she didn't know that she had a visitor. What with dodging the thorns on the waving branches, she had all she could do to hold on to the top of the ladder. Down below stood Mr. Fedora looking up at Mary perched among the flowers and he thought never before had he seen anyone so lovely.

"Hey, there!" he called, tapping his fingers on one of her legs to get her attention.

Startled by this unexpected gesture, Mary turned around quickly, lost her balance and began to fall. Luckily, Johnny caught her in time, and they both landed on the ground in a heap. Mary emerged without a scratch but Johnny was laid out flat as a pancake. When he came around, he not only looked like a pancake, he felt like one. But if he expected sympathy, he was disappointed.

"It's you again!" exclaimed Mary. "Now look what you've done."

Mr. Fedora had narrowly escaped with his life but he did not lose his head.

"Honey chile," he whispered. "Thank all the lucky stars I was there to catch you when you fell."

"Well, whose fault was it?" cried Mary, indignantly.

"Tell the folks back home I died happy and suffered none!" After which shameful bit of skulduggery, he closed his eyes and gave as good an imitation of a dead hero as he knew how.

Johnny was never one to let the dust settle on his good resolutions. He was back that same night with a peace offering in a cellophane wrapper branded with the trade-mark of a famous Dallas firm.

Mary had seen nylons in shop windows and on the legs of other ladies, but she had never actually handled them, and the idea of possessing a pair ranked high on her list of Things That Will Never Happen To Me. If Johnny wanted to get into her good books he had made the right start.

But there is something about nylons that makes some girls want to look round the next corner of a man's mind.

Mary knew, only too well, the kind of girls who wouldn't be caught dead in anything but nylons. "No better than they ought to be," was the village verdict and even the taproom of the Thatchers Arms, more broad-minded in its assessment of human frailties, considered sheer stockings little less than a symbol of shame.

Obviously, she would have to watch her step. No point in possessing nylons if they couldn't be worn. You couldn't put them in a drawer and stroke them all day. There would be no trouble with the Reverend. She might be wearing stockings of any sort for all *he* could tell. But Mrs. Gossop! You wouldn't get away with nylons when she was around. And Mrs. Gossop was always popping in when least expected. Still nylons were nylons. . . .

Mr. Fedora followed this tug-of-war between a lady and her conscience with amused tolerance. "Don't you like them?" he asked.

"I think they're beautiful," admitted Mary. "They must have cost an awful lot."

"Forget it!" said Mr. Fedora. "These things grow on trees at home. Besides, we get things for almost nothing on the Base."

"In that case I guess it's all right," said Mary thanking him.

The first item on Mr. Fedora's schedule was to give those nylons an airing. How about a corner table at the Club with all the proper fixings and a movie to follow, tomorrow night?

Tomorrow! Why, tomorrow there were the petunias to be planted out, the Reverend's supper to be got ready, and the lawn to be mown.

Johnny looked at this slip of a girl with those large, lovely eyes—and those nice legs. "But, honey," he said, "don't you ever have time off for fun?"

"There's a lot to be done," Mary told him, "and no one to do it but me."

"Okay, honey," said Mr. Fedora, "I'll come along and lend a hand with the mowing."

THE VICARAGE garden was becoming a real problem. No harm in letting the shrubbery go, but if something wasn't done about the lawns and the borders they would soon be beyond all hope.

So that, between jobs in the house, Mary always had the garden to fall back upon.

The trouble with the country is that everything happens at the same time. When grass is growing on the lawns it is also growing in the meadows. When a man is needed in the kitchen garden, two men are needed on the farm. And, very properly, the farm comes first.

So the jungle of the countryside was creeping into the gardens of Merriford Vicarage, and the Reverend was in danger of being swamped by its exuberant growth. Only Mary stood between him and complete extinction, but the grass, the borders and the bindweed were getting her down. The end of her losing battle was in sight.

And then came Johnny with his tales of blue ribbons and nights at the fair. If you must be sorry for someone spare a thought for this son of the city. Poor Johnny Fedora, caught up in the summer pageantry of an English garden, knowing nothing of the tragedies that lurk behind the roses round the door. The lawns were large, the grass was long and the old mowing machine was obstinate as a mule. After two hours' strict application to business, the toiler had managed to nibble away a bit of lawn no bigger than the vestry floor.

And did his back ache! All his muscles, it seemed, were in the wrong place. Or was he using an entirely new set which needed a bit of running in?

Gardens! Huh! Is life so lacking in troubles that each one of us can afford to plant a little hell upon his very doorstep? Left to herself, Nature arranges for flowers to grow where they give the best results and cause the least trouble. Consider the lilies of the field. Spare a thought for the moon daisy in the meadow and the ragged robin by the brook. Was Solomon in all his glory arrayed like one of these? No, sir! He was not!

But, instead of being satisfied with this lavish loveliness of the wild, along comes the gardener, deep in his own conceit, and proceeds to improve upon the carefully considered schedule of the Almighty by crowding His flowers into unhealthy reservations where they are at the mercy of every known pest. . . . And when some sturdy, indigenous plant manages to stand upon its own feet the gardener calls it a weed and will have none of it.

And yet, to be fair, when the sun started dropping behind the tall trees and you caught the scent of the sweet briar and the honeysuckle, there might be something to be said for all this nonsense—if only that girl in the cotton frock would stop *working* for a minute.

But there was no need to make such hard work of it. Next night, the Reverend was startled by the outcry of a mechanical contraption which laughed at long grass, hurled itself at molehills, and was guaranteed to cut a lawn in half the time. Mr. Fedora, having borrowed it from the Base gardener, found that it took a bit of handling and was apt to run away with you; but anything was better than tackling the jungle with the derelict old hand machine.

Unfortunately, Johnny didn't know how to stop the darn thing. It was covered with taps and plugs, each with a special function, but the more he operated these mysterious gadgets the louder roared the exhaust and the faster the wheels went round; until Mr. Fedora found himself flying at the tail of the juggernaut, his feet barely touching the ground.

At this point, the Reverend appeared on the scene and attempted to approach the new gardener, so miraculously provided by Providence in answer to his prayers. In the middle of the lawn stood the Vicar of Merriford and round him roared and rattled the cyclonic disturbance ridden and directed by Mr. Fedora, orphan of that particular storm.

"Really," reflected the Reverend, "a very energetic young fellow!" Most gardeners he had known were all too ready to lean upon their spades at the approach of their employers. Whereas this admirable young man would not even pause to pass the time of day. Splendid fellow! If only there were more like him.

And then, luckily for Johnny, the gas gave out and the infernal machine stopped of its own accord—calm followed storm and peace returned to an English garden. True, the Vicarage lawn resembled a rather haphazard crew cut administered by an un-friendly barber at the Base, but much of the grass had gone—and that was something. The Reverend approached warily; Mary crept from behind the bushes and Mr. Fedora tried to look like Paul Revere at the end of his famous ride.

"An excellent contrivance," said the Reverend, administering a benedictory pat to the red-hot engine of the infernal machine. "Just the thing for mowing those difficult mounds in the churchyard, don't you think? Give the young man a cup of tea, Mary; he looks a little warm after all his hard work."

MERRIFORD CHURCH, strangely placed in the middle of a field half a mile from the village, may not compare in size with those lesser cathedrals built by Cotswold wool barons at Northleach and Chipping Campden. The young Shelley did not write an ode to its ethereal spire as he did in Lechlade churchyard; Oliver Cromwell did not stable his horses in its central aisle as he did at Burford; nor is the cast shoe of John O' Gaunt's charger nailed to its church door as it still is at Kempsford. And yet, on a drowsy Sunday evening in summertime, when its bells are calling across the flat meadows. . . .

There has always been magic in the bells of Merriford. For the best part of a thousand years bells have rung out from the old tower, the most recent minor peal having been cast and placed in position in the year 1765. Why they should seem to possess some special virtue it would be hard to say. Possibly the peculiar formation of the Vale gives their notes an added quality. Or were those old bell-founders, two centuries ago, better craftsmen than they knew?

Whatever the answer, there were no bells like the Merriford bells. Crisply on a winter morning, softly on a summer evening, they sent their cheerful challenge or their mild benediction across the quiet countryside. Strangers lured into this land of wet meadows by the winding upper reaches of the Thames, and farm laborers who had never known the inside of their parish church paused for one healing moment to listen to the message of the bells.

At times when the Vicar of Merriford felt the need to buttress his belief in his ministry he took some comfort from this message of the bells. The authority of a parish church cannot be entirely gauged by the number of occupied pews or the size of the offertory. Like the widening circles of a rise in the big trout pool, virtue spreads along the most unexpected channels. Who can doubt the evangelistic influences of church bells heard on a summer evening across the quiet water meadows of the Vale?

Soon after the Americans had fixed their warning flying light to the tower of Merriford church the top sergeant in charge of the working party, happening to meet the Vicar in the village street, asked him if he had been up into his belfry lately. If he hadn't the sooner he took a look round the better. "You Britishers," said the top sergeant, "like things *old*, but those bells have been hanging since the Battle of Lexington and that's too long for timber to carry the weight. Better get someone to give it the once-over, doc."

"Dear me," said the Reverend, "is anything seriously wrong? Don't tell me the timbers . . ."

"Eaten up with dry rot," the top sergeant assured him. "Those bells of yours are liable to fall any minute now."

The Reverend communicated with the diocesan architect who, in due course, issued a report and prepared an estimate for the replacement of the old timber work by a steel and metal frame from which the bells would swing on modern ball bearings. Some financial assistance might be expected from the appropriate diocesan fund, but the bulk of the very considerable expenditure must be raised by public subscription in the parish and surrounding areas.

After an unhappy half-hour with his churchwardens, the Reverend decided to close the belfry at once and to call a church meeting as soon as possible. Not that much financial help was to be expected from that quarter. The Reverend realized that his parishioners would be with him to a man, but he had no illusions as to their financial possibilities, and where all that money was to come from remained one of the great mysteries.

The church meeting, called to consider the problem, was a very solemn affair. There were six parishioners present, including Mary, Mrs. Gossop, and the man who looked after the graveyard on two evenings a week. These with the churchwardens and the Vicar made up the full complement.

The Vicar presided and explained the extent of the disaster that had overwhelmed the parish. He announced that the bells would not be rung again, until further notice, and asked that the tenants of outlying farms should be warned to this effect. Then, after mentioning a figure which made one of the churchwardens whistle, he invited suggestions. None was forthcoming and he was about to refer the matter back to the church council for further consideration when Mrs. Gossop rose.

Mrs. Gossop was, at this time, the only really religious woman in Merriford. She mixed virtue and venom in degrees which varied with the particular prejudice of the moment. When the Vicar's wife died, she had stepped quietly but firmly into the vacant position until the unfortunate man, waking in the morning, was almost surprised not to find her face upon the empty pillow.

But, somehow, this excellent arrangement hadn't seemed to work. The Reverend, perhaps, was a little blind to its obvious advantages but, whatever the reason, Mrs. Gossop had retired behind her white lace window curtains and worked in more mysterious ways her wonders to perform. Now she came out into the open.

Mrs. Gossop rose! They must all, she said, sympathize with their beloved Vicar in his present difficulties but this was no time for mincing words. The needs of the church and the spiritual welfare of the parish came before personal considerations. One could not blind oneself to the fact that this matter of the church bells was merely a *symptom,* and they must probe deeper for causes that had produced such lamentable effects. Mrs. Gossop did not actually claim that heavenly vengeance for human shortcomings had rotted the rafters of the old belfry but she was certainly drifting in that direction.

[85]

Their beloved Vicar, continued Mrs. Gossop, had served them well over a long period of years. He labored, according to his lights, during the toil and heat of the day; and, now that evening had come, was it unfriendly to suggest that he should enjoy the fruits of those labors in quiet retirement, leaving some younger and more physically capable successor to grapple with the difficult problems facing the incumbent of the parish.

If this matter of the church bells, said Mrs. Gossop, were placed in its right perspective, it was reasonable to ask how things had been allowed to come to such a pass. One had only to read the printed notice above the collection box to learn that the old timber work in the belfry had been in position for the past two hundred years. This was an elm country and elm could not be expected to withstand the ravages of time as oak rafters might have done.

Meanwhile, whatever the regrettable reasons, some-one was faced with the stupendous task of reconditioning this House of God; surely a crippling burden to place upon the shoulders of one whose working days must be so nearly done. As she had said, the sprritual welfare of the parish came before personal considerations; and, she did not doubt that her old friend and pastor would be the first to appreciate the motives that had prompted her to move in the matter.

"Are you moving a resolution?" asked the Reverend, mildly.

"No," replied Mrs. Gossop. "I merely wish to clear the air for any future discussion."

"Very kind of you," said the old man. "I will pass on your extremely practical suggestions to my churchwardens."

To say that Mrs. Gossop had dropped a bombshell into the meeting would be quite untrue. Only the Reverend could make any sense of her rigmarole. Mary had a vague idea that Mrs. G. was up to her tricks again; the two churchwardens reckoned she was blowing off steam—talking for the sake of talking as you might say; and the verger-gravedigger was asleep.

But the Vicar of Merriford sensed the challenge: "Get Out—This Means You!" was the burden of Mrs. Gossop's song. She had coated the pill with a certain amount of sugar, but the attack was well-timed and the poison would sink in.

12

THE DEFECTION of Mr. Fedora did not pass unnoticed at the American Air Base. All his familiar haunts were searched in vain. The taproom of the Thatchers Arms was drawn blank. Saturday night dances were combed for one who had been the life and soul of the party.

Summer evenings came and went; English cornfields were turning from green to gold; very soon the spindleberries would color the hedgerows with their coral pink—and still Johnny Fedora was as one who had never been.

But in the Vicarage garden the birds were still singing.

There is something to be said for coming suddenly round a corner and seeing an English garden for the first time—as Johnny Fedora had done. In England, it seemed, you surrounded a garden with the secrecy reserved for a top-secret atom bomber at the Base. You protected it with high walls and thick hedges—anything, in fact, to prevent other people from joining in the fun. Highly comical, thought Mr. Fedora, picturing a garden world in which dahlias and delphiniums were defended to the death behind parapets and barbed wire entanglements.

But, after an evening or two in the quiet Vicarage garden, he began to get the idea lurking behind all this nonsense. These barriers between you and the outside world lost their unfriendliness.

The funny thing about gardening, Mr. Fedora discovered, was that the job seemed to grow on you. You started off hating every minute of it, but once you had worked the aches out of your back, you almost got to like it.

Even mowing the lawn, on some warm summer evening, had something to be said for it—a pleasant rhythm followed by a quiet sense of achievement. And how old it was and what things it had seen! Before Johnny had been in the garden a week, he had learned to love a lawn.

Nothing, of course, to do with this girl with the large eyes and the urchin crop, who ran the big house single-handed, mothered an old man and had no time for fun and games. Mr. Fedora was still capable of persuading himself that he loved a garden for a garden's sake; and Mary, deeply immersed in her own affairs, did nothing to disillusion him. So the nylon stockings remained packed away in a drawer and the bright lights were as far away as ever.

The only trouble was that the Reverend got caught up in the prevailing enthusiasm for better and brighter borders. He would come wandering out of his study when he should have been preparing next Sunday's sermons—"like an old bumble bee," to quote Mr. Fedora's unspoken thought—and three people, even in the large Vicarage garden, were as large a crowd as three people have always been.

This awkward situation was aggravated by the fact that the Reverend had taken rather a liking to his young visitor and seemed always anxious to consult him on certain aspects of Anglo-American relations, a subject about which Mr. Fedora could not care less.

Was it true, asked the Reverend, that American children educated in English schools would find themselves handicapped on their return to their own country? He had seen it stated that there were no equivalent standards permitting a satisfactory exchange of students; and that the authorities at the Air Base had decided to open a school to be staffed by teachers imported from the United States. Was this, in Mr. Fedora's opinion, a wise move or did Mr. Fedora agree that the contacts made by American children attending English schools might bring about a greater international harmony in later years? What did Mr. Fedora think?

Mr. Fedora having no opinions on such academic problems, the Reverend passed on to where Mary was dismantling the derelict herbaceous border.

"Mary," he asked, "how much are we paying that young fellow from the Aerodrome?"

"Nothing," said Mary.

"Why not?" asked the Reverend.

"Because he isn't worth it," said Mary.

"Then why employ him?"

"I don't," said Mary. "He just comes."

"You must tell him not to come again."

"That won't stop him," said Mary. "But what's wrong with him working for nothing if he wants to?"

"It places us under an obligation," explained the Reverend. "After all, a laborer is worthy of his hire."

"Not this laborer," Mary assured him. "You'd have

to pay him in farthings—and even then you'd be out of pocket!"

The old man smiled. It seemed the lady did protest too much. "Very well, Mary," he said. "I will speak to the young man myself. We can't have him hanging round the place to no purpose."

"He doesn't worry *me*," said Mary. "If the poor fellow thinks he's helping, why not let him go on thinking? And he's company—of a sort."

"I shall speak to him," said the Reverend. "We can't have any misunderstanding. Why do you suppose he comes here night after night?"

"I can't think!" said Mary.

Johnny saw that the "old bumble bee" was coming back and pretended to be working double tides, but that dodge didn't work.

"Tell me," said the Reverend, "what is it about a garden that appeals to you, particularly? One doesn't, as a rule, find young fellows of your age bothering about flowers."

Johnny raised his eyes to the heavens as though calling on all the angels to bear witness. "It's the *quiet*," he said. "After all that noise up at the Base— nothing but talk, talk, talk; nothing but dames and dancing. And then to come here and not to have to listen to the sound of a human voice!"

The Reverend smiled. "Don't let my little house-keeper intrude on your meditations," he said.

"Oh, *that* dame!" sniffed Mr. Fedora.

That was how matters stood in the Vicarage garden until the bees swarmed and upset everything.

The solitary bee hive in the far corner of the orchard was the only thing that Mary didn't manage. Mary didn't like bees. If it hadn't been that the Reverend thought they were good for the garden, she would have turned them out long ago. As it was, she pushed them into the far corner of the orchard and tried to forget they were there.

The postman, on the other hand, adored bees. He would come along in his little red van, pick up the afternoon collection, have a cup of tea with the jolly postmistress and then find some excuse to trot down the Vicarage orchard and see how his beloved bees were getting on.

As a civil servant, he was a bit of a bureaucrat and admired the controlled planning of their welfare state—a trifle regimented one might say. But it was a satisfying well-ordered way of life, taken all in all. He did not inquire too deeply into the feelings of the bees, themselves. It was true they lost all their savings, but they received sugar subsidies during the winter;

and, if they seemed dissatisfied, he could always give them a whiff of smoke from his little bellows.

Sometimes, when things got too hot, they would try to emigrate. In that case, the postman shook the swarm into an old skep, dusted them with a little flour and pushed them back into another hive.

The bees were only troublesome when there was thunder in the air. They were terrified of thunder, and, as a frightened bee is as dangerous as a frightened human being, you had to look out for yourself when there was thunder about. Even the postman left them alone when an angry drumming inside the hive warned him that they were on the warpath.

But, on a warm day in late July, through carelessness or the absence of official business, he planned his annual raid for an afternoon when the bees were in no mood to be robbed of their life's savings. So that, later in the evening, a flight of warrior bees, returning from an offensive sortie, dive-bombed an enemy emplacement—which happened to be Mary.

Never has beauty in distress called more loudly for her knight in shining armor and never has that knight responded more nobly to the call. But this wasn't one of those simple jobs like scaling a fortress or slaying a dragon. Did *you* ever try to part a honey bee from the hair of a honey blonde?

By the time Johnny had got his bee, comforted the

unhappy lady and kissed her tears away, the shadows of the apple trees were lengthening in the Vicarage orchard; and the Reverend was beginning to wonder what had happened to Mary.

When would she be coming in to draw the blinds and bring him some of the hot scones and new honey she had promised him for his supper?

THE BELLS of Merriford had been silent for a month and no steps had yet been taken to set them ringing again—apart from an Appeal to stray visitors, in the Vicar's shaky handwriting. This appeared on the church notice board between the latest Voters' List and a roster of ladies responsible for the altar flowers.

The Reverend was completely stunned by the disaster: twenty times a day he asked himself where the money was to come from; and long, sleepless hours found him pondering the same problem. It was one thing to hold a garden fête for new cushions, or a whist drive to balance the organ fund, but how did one set about raising the large capital sum for which his handful of parishioners appeared to be responsible?

It would have been different in the old days. Fifty years ago, one would have called at half-a-dozen big houses and have come away with the money; but the big houses, the big benefactors and the old sense of obligation didn't exist any more.

Those were the days when great industrialists from the towns were buying great estates and learning to be country gentlemen. They inherited the manor pew and with it the manorial rights and obligations of the old squires. The Reverend had felt rather like one of those jolly old highwaymen; robbing only the rich and sparing poor men's goods; bidding these wealthy ones "stand and deliver, in the name of the Lord!"

And they rather liked you for it; welcomed the opportunity to buy themselves into their new position. There would be a bit of friendly banter over the luncheon table at the big house; and, after protesting his poverty, the new squire would return flourishing a fat cheque which he was careful to lay business side up on the damask tablecloth.

No going to *them* with your hat in your hand. A little polite resistance—to mark the value of the concession—but no loss of face on the part of the suppliant. The money had to be found and there was only one place to look for it. Heaven help the ambitious upstart who tried to bounce his way to the top of the subscription list; or, the neighbouring nabob who came poaching into another fellow's preserves. When your people in the back pews prayed for those who were put in authority over them, they knew what they were talking about and you couldn't let them down.

But not today. Two wars and crippling taxation had altered all that. Out of the incidence of surtax a strange anomaly had been born—the more you had, the less you had. Those old family mansions were millstones about the necks of their unlucky owners who could neither staff them, rent them, nor even give them away.

So mused the Reverend, passing those old happy hunting grounds in unhappy review. One big house was now an approved school, another the fine new offices of the local Rural District Council, and the third a convalescent home. Yet another had been split up into flats, sold separately to unfriendly neighbours who lived uneasy lives on a common doorstep.

How did one cope with such a situation—how to get the bells of Merriford ringing again?

The Reverend was at his wits' end. He still believed that running a country parish was an old man's job, but he knew in his heart that he was evading the main issue. The real challenge to his ministry came from those rotten rafters in the old belfry; and, until he got his church bells ringing again, their very silence condemned him as an old man no longer equal to his trust.

It almost seemed that Mrs. Gossop had been right when she held a pistol to his head and told him to get out! Were others saying the same things about him behind his back? Was his spiritual armor so rusted that he was no longer fit to take the field? It almost seemed so.

But even running away had its problems. What would be said of a soldier who resigned his commission in face of a sudden emergency or of a doctor who decided to retire from practice in the middle of a dangerous epidemic? All very puzzling; it seemed you would be wrong whatever you did.

And what would happen to Mary? In another year or two, she would have been old enough to marry some nice young fellow and to have had a nice home of her own; but, if they had to leave the

Vicarage she would drift back into domestic service and that would be the end of her.

Mrs. Gossop would have had no regrets on that score. She had never really approved of Mary, particularly since that silly little quarrel over Scrap. But Mrs. Gossop was always having a silly little quarrel with somebody.

Scrap was almost a Sealyham, a gay little dog combining the best qualities of the corgi, the border terrier and others of his more remote ancestors.

But it was the touch of Scottie in him that caused all the trouble.

Scrap really liked biting people. Not, you understand, from any feeling of malice—quite the reverse. He only bit people he liked, and as he liked almost everybody, he was always biting somebody. After all, what is a bite more or less between friends?

Scrap adored the postman. They were such friends that the postman was almost afraid to go down the orchard to look at the bees—until he bought a pair of the Major's old spats at the rummage sale to protect his ankles.

All the errand boys got bitten. Scrap would sit in the middle of the Vicarage drive, giving his famous imitation of a lion about to spring; and, if one of the boys got by without being bitten, he would brag about it for weeks.

The thing became such a public scandal that the village policeman called at the Vicarage to lodge an unofficial complaint.

"Now, Miss Mary," he said, "as you know I'm the last to cause any trouble. 'Live and let live' is my motto, but that makes seven people your dog has bitten this week. One of these days, you mark my words, that dog is going to bite the wrong person and then the fat *will* be in the fire."

"What will they do to Scrap?" asked Mary.

"Put him on the scrap heap," said the policeman, who was a large, cheerful man with a rare sense of humour—as the word is understood in country parts. "There'll be a funeral and you'll be chief mourner."

"Scrap doesn't mean any harm," said Mary.

"Not an ounce of vice in him," agreed constable Large, "but how are you going to prove it? Why not keep him tied up for a bit?"

Mary had tied Scrap to the handle of the back door. But his bark proved so much worse than his bite, that the law stepped in again, and warned her that she was committing a public nuisance and must release the animal at once.

Scrap was a happy little dog, only one sorrow clouded his young life: he had never bitten Mrs. Gossop. But one day, when the sun was shining and all the smells were good, even Mrs. Gossop couldn't spoil the fun. And so she got bitten, the same as everybody else.

Mrs. Gossop couldn't take a joke. She went straight off to the county police headquarters, insisted on seeing the Superintendent, and told him such a tale of terror as he had never heard. A dangerous dog was entirely out of control; it had bitten everybody; not a moment was to be lost. If the police were afraid to move in the matter she would herself approach the Home Office and her Member of Parliament.

Evidently, the lady meant business. The Superintendent was most polite and promised immediate action. On inquiry he found that Constable Large, was on holiday. So he called in a promising young subordinate new to the area, and packed him off to Merriford to collect evidence in support of any possible charge.

"Don't run any unnecessary risks," said the Superintendent. "Get the names of the people it has bitten and take statements in the worst cases. The woman seemed a bit hysterical and may have been exaggerating, but it sounds serious. Get busy!"

When the police car drove into Merriford, a deep calm pervaded the village street. The men were away in the fields; the Thatchers Arms was not yet open; the women were cooking, and the voices of children singing hymns in the little school lent a touch of almost Sabbath melancholy to the peaceful scene. Only the Reverend in his black cassock, on his way to take the weekly scripture class, moved across the bright landscape—rather like a bewildered fly lost in the middle of a large white tablecloth. At his heels, a small and rather nondescript terrier trailed demurely like an attendant acolyte.

The young police officer stopped his car and waited for the old gentleman to come alongside. "Excuse me," he said, "this *is* Merriford, isn't it?"

"Yes," replied the Reverend, "this is Merriford."

"Funny!" said the policeman. "It seems quiet enough."

"What did you expect?" smiled the old man.

"We received information at headquarters that you were having trouble with a mad dog."

"How very odd!" said the Reverend. "Some practical joker, perhaps?"

"Not much of a joke for someone," muttered the policeman grimly. "Sorry to have troubled you, padre!"

"Not at all!" said the Reverend, "but you must

excuse me . . . I'm a little late, already. Come along, Scrap!"

"So the woman sent us on a wild-goose chase," said the Superintendent. "Very well, I'll have her along and talk to her."

When Mrs. Gossop received an official invitation to call at police headquarters, with the added courtesy of a car placed at her disposal, she put on her best bonnet, and was all set for another happy interview with that nice man who was so polite on the occasion of her first visit. The happy interview went something like this:

"Good morning, madam. Please sit down. Before taking any official action I felt we might have a little private chat. Am I right in supposing that in lodging your complaint you were not confining yourself to a personal charge?"

"Quite right!" agreed Mrs. Gossop. "I wished to draw attention to a long-standing public nuisance."

"You do not propose taking personal action against the owner of the animal?"

"Certainly not!" said Mrs. Gossop. "I was merely setting the law in motion in order that justice might be done."

"You feel the situation is so serious that it demands the intervention of the police?"

"Quite so!" agreed Mrs. Gossop. "What else are you here for?"

"We have been at some pains to check up on your information. I sent a personal representative to make inquiries."

"Naturally!" murmured Mrs. Gossop.

"He reports that he can find nothing to substantiate, in the slightest degree, the extravagant charges you have laid before me."

"The man's mad!" gasped Mrs. Gossop. "He should be dismissed from the force! A clear case of corruption."

"He failed to find a single individual who was prepared to lodge a complaint or to give evidence for the prosecution. There would be no witnesses to call and no case to answer. The defendant would be discharged and the prosecution would be very properly criticized for wasting the time of the court. Good morning, madam."

"You refuse to take any action?" said Mrs. Gossop. "At least, I have a right to know what inquiries you made, if any, before arriving at such a ridiculous decision. You must have approached *some* responsible person?"

"We did, indeed, but investigations at this stage are naturally confidential. However, if you press the point, I have a letter here from Major O'Beirne."

The Superintendent opened a correspondence file and read: "This Gossop woman is a blazing nuisance. Always has been. You can tell her so from me. If she weren't so tough, I would have bitten her myself long ago!"

They could expect no mercy from Mrs. Gossop after that little affair, and, however unpopular Mrs. Gossop might be, she was a force to be reckoned with.

The Reverend closed his eyes and wondered what life without Merriford would mean for him. People thought of retirement as a grateful laying aside of burdens too heavy to be borne. They pictured you revelling in your newly-found freedom; finding time at last to do all the things you had always longed to do. How wrong they were!

A few of his older parishioners would be sorry to see him go. For a time, the new man would be compared unfavorably with the old parson, until things settled down and the village got quietly into its stride again.

They would get rid of the rambling old Vicarage, cut it up into flats or sell it for a preparatory school. The new man would be given a villa on a council building estate—until the living was absorbed by a neighboring parish and the last trace of his fifty years' ministry was swept away.

And he, the late Vicar of Merriford, would go to Cheltenham or Bath to join those other old men, who pottered up and down the promenade, filling in the unprofitable hours over a cup of coffee or the shelves of a private lending library. Until strange men wheeled him away to the municipal crematorium, and he was taken up to heaven in a pillar of undertaker's fire.

The Reverend was a man of simple faith and simple tastes. His heaven was no city set on a great and high mountain, having walls of jasper and foundations garnished with all manner of precious stones. Rather, it was the heaven he knew—a land of wet water meadows, narrow country lanes and deep ditches, glorious in summer-time with marsh marigolds and meadowsweet.

> *Alone with the grayling and his God—*
> *And a fishing rod.*

FOR SOME DAYS past there had been strange go-
ings-on in the Vicarage orchard. Sitting in his study,
the Reverend could hear squeals, screams and
shouted instructions which made him think that one
of the village boys had fallen into the river.

Then, just as he had recovered from one shock,
there would be a crash followed by such a commotion
that he could only suppose someone had knocked
over a beehive and was being stung to death.

Actually, it was Mary learning to ride a bicycle,

assisted by Mr. Fedora, who, having borrowed a service machine from the Base, had selected the slope
down to the river as a promising practice ground.

When the Reverend appeared at the back door,
the course of instruction had reached the stage when
the co-pilot releases his hold of the controls and his
pupil becomes air-borne. Away went the bicycle,
closely followed by Scrap, barking furiously, and only
a friendly apple tree saved Mary from a ducking in
the Thames.

All this activity had been started by Mr. Fedora's
ridiculous statement that the Thames, England's
great national river, had nothing on his own Rio
Grande. Mr. Fedora had even gone so far as to claim
that, compared to the Rio Grande, the Thames was
"a no-account little creek" that did not amount to
a trickle. This silly nonsense had so upset Mary that
she wouldn't have him in the Vicarage garden for the
rest of the week.

When his patriotic fervor had cooled, Johnny
appeared at the back door and ate large helpings of
humble pie. He had been all wrong in his geograph-
ical surmises. It was the Rio Grande that was a no-
account creek. Compared to the Thames, the Rio
Grande was little better than a duck-pond. The mis-
take was due to the fact that his education was limited
to the grades and geography was not a required sub-

ject. Would Miss Mary improve his mind on such matters? Would she take him on a pilgrimage to the source of England's mighty river? Johnny could secure two bicycles.

Mary had never found time in her busy life to learn to ride a bicycle, but this shameful admission did not worry Mr. Fedora at all. In that case he would teach her—and the very next evening the course of instruction had begun.

Wednesday was the Day of Pilgrimage. That day was chosen because the Major would be paying his weekly call at the Vicarage and could keep the Reverend company while Mary was away. A white mist spangling the spiders' webs gave certain promise of a sweet Autumn day. Mary was placed reverently on the seat of the bicycle, and off they started to find the source of a river that made the Rio Grande look like a duck-pond.

They rode out into the silver morning like Chaucer's pilgrims on their way to Canterbury—along winding lanes, down drowsy village streets, past cottage gardens so tightly packed with flowers that each might have been a Victorian posy. They peeped into tiny churchyards with fading memories of John, "who sweetly fell asleep in Jesus" and of Ann, "relict of the said John." And so they came at last to the point where their adventures really began.

The trouble about the Thames is that while the actual stream is common to all, the fields through which it flows are private property. You may sit in a boat and fish forever, but you may not sit on the banks and fish for five minutes. Indeed, you may not sit on the banks—fishing or no fishing—unless you happen to know a friendly farmer or join an anglers' club that has taken over his fishing rights. All very confusing!

How did you discover the source of a river when you were not allowed to set foot upon its banks? The two pilgrims were debating this problem when a group of lesser pilgrims—six small boys and a home-made fishing rod—turned into the field, marched boldly along the river bank, and settled down to fish.

It so happened that an honest angler had already settled down on the same promising pitch; and, round him, the small boys draped themselves, intent on sharing the benefits which he enjoyed. For what saith the Compleat Angler in his discourse on the contemplative man's recreation: "If common anglers should attend you, and be eye-witnesses of the success, not of your fortune but of your skill, it would doubtless beget in them an emulation to be like you, and that emulation might beget an industrious diligence to be so."

Unfortunately, the small boys soon tired of the

pleasant curiosity of fishing, and started to disturb the honest angler's recreation by throwing stones at his float. Angered by their action, he informed them that the fishing rights on that reach of the river were strictly preserved by his Club, and that if they didn't make themselves scarce he would have the law on them.

The small boys replied that this was Mr. Akers' meadow and they would fish as they pleased.

The honest angler explained the niceties of fishing rights in general and the strength of his own legal position in particular.

The small boys were not impressed. They knew nothing of Fishing Clubs. Mr. Akers was their god and in him they put their trust.

Then, said the honest angler, would they get on with their fishing and stop throwing stones at his float!

The small boys informed him, in chorus, that they " 'ad lorst their 'ook, mister."

The honest angler saw a gleam of hope shining through a break in the clouds. If he gave them sixpence to buy a new hook, would they depart and buy one, leaving him to fish in peace?

They would, and trailed away along the river bank. But in two minutes they were back again.

"We've found our 'ook, mister!" they said.

Whereupon the honest angler bade farewell to his pleasant hours and departed, "even as a shadow that passeth away and returns not."

The moral of this little story was not lost upon our two pilgrims. But their bicycles, like the poet's donkey, had no wings with which to fly the hedges and barbed wire fences that ran down to the river bank, and they were forced to return to the road.

The nearer they got to the source the more difficult their quest became; the brooks were so large and the actual river so small that it was almost impossible to tell it from its tributaries. Where it crossed the road between Ewen and Kemble it was quite a little fellow, just one mile long.

And here they began to taste the thrill of all explorers as they neared their goal. Somewhere within sight of Kemble Steeple was the end of their pilgrimage: England's historic heritage—Trewsbury Mead, the true source of the Thames. But, as with the storming of Everest, the last hundred yards were to provide the real crux of the problem.

Round which corner, over which stile, across which meadow was the birthplace of Britain's national river to be found? Johnny asked everybody but they all seemed to think it didn't matter. The river itself, now no wider than a wash tub, went dwindling away through a bramble hedge where none could follow.

King Canute might have sailed his fleet as far up as Cricklade, but he certainly didn't reach the top of the Thames.

After riding round in circles for the better part of an hour they found an old, old man leaning against a gate, and stopped to talk to him. "Yes," he said. "I been livin' in these parts all my days, nigh on ninety year, I have. When I wur a bwoy I had heard summat about a river of sorts as started thereabouts, but that wur a long time ago, afore the old Queen died. No river there nowadays, not as I knowed on. Only ditches and suchlike, none on 'em fit to float a sprat."

Leaving this unhelpful museum piece propped up against his gate-post, they climbed the great ridge of the Roman Road where the old Fosse Way runs; and here Mr. Fedora decided that if he had failed to find the source of the Thames, he had certainly discovered the Heart of England. For he was looking down into that cradle of all good things, bounded on one side by the Berkshire Downs and on the other by the Cotswold Hills.

Here are to be found those little limestone villages that seem so sad on dull, unfriendly days, and are so happy when the sun is shining—those little, laughing rivers with lovely English names: Coln, Leach, Windrush and tiny Dickler which "crowds more beauty into its few miles than any other Gloucestershire river for twice its length." And here also can be seen those amazing thirteenth and fourteenth-century tithe barns which, "having withstood the catastrophes of time, can still put great cathedrals to shame by reason of their dignity, their valor and their greatness."

Mr. Fedora could not have described the panorama in such intimate detail but he, somehow, felt the wonder of it all. Some Americans still feel their roots tugging at them from such scenes as this; other Americans have aped things English as a passing whim, but here was an American who, for one magical moment, would have died for England.

Seeing him stand there so quietly, Mary thought that he was disappointed. "I'm sorry, Johnny," she said, "I thought it would've been bigger than that."

Mr. Fedora shook himself free of this flock of daydreams that had come floating up out of the Vale.

"Sorry for what?" he asked.

"Dragging you all that way along all those roads to find the start of the Thames."

"Oh, the *Thames!* Forget it!" And then Mr. Fedora did a most surprising thing. He took Mary in his arms and, for no particular reason, kissed her and kissed her until the two of them were caught as nearly between crying and laughing as made no difference.

They discovered the source when they had forgotten to worry about it. A friendly young fellow, driv-

ing a combine harvester along the Roman Road
explained its mysteries. "In wet summers," he said,
"it starts over on the left side of the Fosse and trickles
down through Mr. John Phillips' field on the right.
In dry summers such as this one, it starts at the big
spring by that windmill you can just see in a dead
line with Kemble steeple."

"Thank you for your trouble," said Johnny.

"Don't mention it! Only too pleased. It starts small,
but they tell me it gets bigger farther down!" The big
contraption toiled over the brow of the hill and he
was gone.

So they walked across to the second field and found
the baby Thames bubbling out of a very ordinary
hole in the ground. No noise and no nonsense; no
sculptured Mother Isis, no goddess of the river with
a bunch of grapes in her lap, as you will find at the
source of the Seine in that valley of the Côte d'Or.

"All very English," thought Mr. Fedora, "to make
so little fuss about such a big thing." The two explorers took off their shoes and stockings and paddled
in the ice-cold, crystal-clear water which barely covered their ankles. After a few yards, they were
stopped by a stone wall in which five holes had been
made to let the water trickle through—the first bridge
over the Thames!

The sun was dropping behind the ridge and the

tall elms were throwing great shadows across the grass before they made a move for home. Sitting by the old Roman Road, Mary had learned a lot of the strange place "back home," to which Johnny would be going when his three years in England were up. Not quite the picture she had imagined. No bandits holding up the stage coach at Bitter Creek: no bad men riding madly in a cloud of dust; no Cisco Kid firing from the hip. Just a wonderful country, so large you could put the whole of England into a corner of it. Perhaps Johnny would take her back home with him. A little frightening, all those miles from Merriford, but Johnny would be there to look after her and that was all that mattered.

And then Mary fell headlong out of her land of dreams. Three years was a long time to wait—anything could happen in three years. Suppose something happened to the Reverend. Suppose she had to go away from Merriford and never saw Johnny any more.

MAJOR TALBOT O'BEIRNE, late of the Inniskilling Dragoons, was the lowest of God's creatures. He drank, he gambled, and he swore. Definitely a poor type—if you judged a man by Mrs. Gossop's standards.

Major O'Beirne was an Irishman on good drinking terms with everybody in Merriford. He existed on an inadequate pension eked out by precarious investments which yielded up their fruits at uncertain seasons. On one occasion, following an unhappy flutter on the Stock Exchange, he had failed to appear at the Thatchers Arms for a month; but his life had been saved by the village milkman who had substituted, each morning, a bottle of stout for the usual ration.

This unworthy specimen the Reverend selected to advise him in his financial difficulties!

The two men had been thrown together by force of circumstances. Existence in a rural village does not bristle with conversational thrills. Successful men complain that life is lonely at the top. If they lived at the top of the Thames they might have something to grumble about.

Coming fresh to Merriford, the Major bought the funny little house at the end of the village, and waited for something to happen. Sickening at last for the sound of a friendly voice, the Irishman had been forced to call at the Vicarage where he had found the Reverend trying to lure a cannibal trout from its hole with a dead bleak. Sitting on the river bank, he had watched this strange proceeding, and, from such small beginnings, a mutual tolerance and respect had ripened with the years.

Not that the Major ever made much of a fisherman. The Thames trout had him beaten from the start, but an occasional chub kept his interest in angling alive, and you would usually find him somewhere along the river bank during the dead hours between closing and opening times at the Thatchers Arms.

The Major had no money and was no churchgoer, yet the Reverend turned to him for succor and support. Angling, like adversity, makes strange bedfellows.

Every Wednesday evening, as regular as clockwork, the Irishman would wobble up the Vicarage drive on his rusty old bicycle, and for the next three hours the two old cronies would talk the sun down the sky—the Major expatiating in his incredible brogue on the political situation, or the Reverend trying to wean him from his evil ways.

Tonight, the Reverend fired his usual opening shot: "I didn't notice you in church on Sunday, Major. Nothing wrong I hope?"

" 'Tis the weight of meself on my game leg," countered the Irishman. "What can you expect with your sacred edifice set in the centre of a great field, miles from anywhere?"

The Major had something there. Back in the Middle Ages when the Black Death ravaged England, the original hamlet of Merriford had been wiped out, and a succeeding generation, led by their parish priest, had wisely established themselves on slightly higher ground—leaving the church standing, as the

Major had truly observed, in the middle of a great field.

"And what sort of a religion," continued the Irishman, "is that which throws a man's temp'ry backslidings in his teeth when the poor wretch is crawling out of the bog of iniquity? Small wonder they've been after putting a red warning light on the tower of the little church set in its great field. Small wonder the bells has stopped calling the lonely traveller to the house of God. . . ."

This was the opening for which the Reverend had been waiting. "Suppose I told you, Major, that we may never hear the bells of Merriford ring again in our lifetime? When the Americans climbed the tower. . . ."

"I knew it!" gasped the Major. "Sitting there beside the sweet waters, listening for the silver bells to shine across the meadows, I said to myself: 'Mother of God,' I said. 'And what has those Americans been up to now?' I said. 'Not content with keeping us awake half the night,' I said. 'And drinking all the whiskey they can lay their hands on,' I said. 'Now they must steal the very church bells to melt down for their infernal machines,'" I said.

"No fault of the Americans," said the Reverend. "The bells of Merriford are our own affair. The timbers in the old belfry are crumbling to dust and if you were to die tomorrow I wouldn't dare to have the big bell tolled for your funeral."

This gloomy prospect brought the Irishman up with a jerk. Robbed of his native rhetoric he became a reasonable human being. If it was only money they wanted they could have his last penny. " 'Tis the end of the quarter and there's something owing here and yonder, but that's not lost that a friend gets. How much will you be needing, Father?" he asked.

"Two thousand pounds," said the Reverend.

The Major sat back and surveyed him with a rheumy eye. "Holy Mother of Jesus!" he gasped. "Is there so much money in the wide world? And if I happen not to have such a trifling amount in my pocket at the moment—what then?"

"I hoped you might be able to advise me," said the old man. "I'm a little out of my depth. . . ."

Having blown off a necessary amount of steam, Major O'Beirne allowed himself to face up to the Reverend's dilemma. His personal financial assistance was considered briefly and dismissed by both parties. Any mortgage on his house had been anticipated. Winning a football pool could not be depended upon. The Stock Exchange, owing to that unfortunate flutter, was no present help in this time of trouble, and the fine new dress suit he had bought back in the twenties had the moth in it. Petty cash realized 15 shillings; there was nothing in the stamp account, and he was afraid to poke his nose inside the bank until he had wiped out his overdraft.

Major Talbot O'Beirne, late of the Inniskilling Dragoons was badly in the red. Financially, he was a washout.

His solitary assets were a fine store of optimism which made Mr. Micawber look like something out of the Book of Job, and the old family motto: "Face the sun and all the shadows will fall behind you."

But he had a heart of gold and the Reverend had acted on a sure instinct when he leaned upon this broken reed. At the end of an hour's discussion, he felt oddly comforted, though nothing tangible had emerged to ease the situation.

"And suppose the incredible amount is not forthcoming," asked the Major. "What then?"

"Then I should have to consider resigning the living in favor of a younger and more active man."

The Irishman rose slowly to his feet and hobbled to the door. "Mary! Mary, me dear!" he shouted. "Dial 999 and ask for the ambulance."

Mary, just back from exploring the source of the Thames, came running. "It's the poor old parson," the Major told her.

"What's wrong with him?" asked Mary.

"He's gone mad, raving mad," said the Major.

Mary was used to the Irishman's funny ways.

"*He's* not the mad one," she said. "If I call the ambulance it isn't the Reverend they'll take to the loony bin. What have you been doing to him this time?"

" 'Tis the church bells," whispered the Major. "The poor old fellow is sick in the head with the worry of it. His talk is all of resigning and handing over to a younger man."

Mary gave a little gasp and went so white that the Major thought she was going to faint. So it had happened at last—just as everything was going so well. They would have to leave the Vicarage and once again she would be alone in the world. No real home, no garden, no Reverend to care for. No Scrap playing at being a lion and biting the errand boys. No Johnny! Mary closed the study door, ran down the stone passage and turned her face to the kitchen wall.

The Major watched her go, before turning to where the old clergyman was sitting in the chair that had harbored him for the past fifty years.

For some reason this peaceful picture infuriated the big Irishman. It was always the same. The tragedies of youth were accepted as little troubles that would pass—but what had this old man to lose compared with the young girl crying her heart out at the end of the passage?

Major Talbot O'Beirne crossed the worn carpet and shook the Vicar of Merriford by the shoulder.

The Reverend looked up in gentle surprise to find the Irishman glowering at him from under his bushy eyebrows. "Dear me," he said, "is anything the matter?"

This mild appraisal of the situation was too much for the Major. "Is anything the matter?" he echoed. "Sure, he sits there and he asks, 'Is anything the matter.' What sort of a Christian soldier would it be who sat in an armchair, leavin' his fellows to fight the Lord's battles—tell me that, will ye? Tell me that!"

"What do you want me to do?" asked the bewildered Reverend.

"Put on that shining armor," replied the Irishman. "Fight the good fight for the glory of God and the little silver bells that shine across the meadows. What sort of a man is it would faint and fear for the sake of a paltry two thousand pounds, will you tell me that?"

"The money must be found," the Reverend reminded him.

"Glory be to God," groaned the Irishman. "He talks as one who had the ruling of the universe and all the weight of the world on his shoulders. Him, no more than a poor little corporal in the mighty army of the Lord. Sound the loud clarion, man, and forward into battle go!"

"There is still the money," persisted the Reverend.

"Practice what you preach," said Major Talbot O'Beirne. "The Lord will provide."

Up in her little room, Mary prayed herself sick; and then, having as little faith as the rest of us, cried herself to sleep. For she knew, none better, what leaving the old Vicarage would mean for her.

MARY'S POSITION at the Vicarage was unusual to say the least of it. She worked like a scrubwoman but she was her own mistress and had some standing in the village. "My little housekeeper," the Reverend had called her, with something of a twinkle in his eye, and she had established herself firmly in that important post. So that today she was "Miss Mary" to most of the old biddies, and heaven help the cheeky errand boy who did not treat her with proper respect.

But once they had left the Vicarage these advantages would disappear. She would have to go into service with someone like Mrs. Gossop and become an ordinary no-account girl or go away altogether. In which case Johnny would be lost to her forevermore.

Everything now depended on getting the bells ringing again. Each morning the villagers looked across the fields to see if the old tower was still standing, and the silence on Sunday evenings was hardly to be borne. No one knew when to start getting ready for church and someone was always being late because there was no "five minute tinkler" to hurry them over the last hundred yards.

Bells, bells, bells—people seemed to think and talk of nothing else. There had been no passing bell when old Mrs. Vardon died, and when Kitty Frost got married it was more like a funeral than a wedding.

Bells, bells, bells—there were folk in the parish who had never bothered about the bells until they stopped ringing. Now, every time the Reverend poked his nose outside the Vicarage gate, they were after him like a pack of hyenas; plaguing him with silly questions and driving the poor man to distraction.

There were one or two, like Mrs. Gossop, who were really nasty about it. Mrs. Gossop never missed a chance to rub it in, as though it was the Reverend's fault that those rotten timbers in the belfry might give way any minute.

Bells, bells, bells—sometimes the old man sat in his

chair on Sunday evening waiting for the chimes to start. Then, on a week day, he would fancy he could hear them ringing and it was all Mary could do to stop him going across to the church and getting into his surplice. If this went on much longer he really would be taken away in an ambulance as the Major had foretold.

Mary had never heard of Edgar Allan Poe, but at night the damnable iteration of imaginary bells wailed like a phantom banshee against the background of her unhappy dreams. Unless something happened soon, there would be two of them taken away on the Major's ambulance.

The real trouble was that the Reverend kept all his troubles to himself. Strange letters in long envelopes would be read several times and put carefully away in the bottom drawer of the old bureau. Sometimes she would find him going through the church accounts to see what could be spared for the Special Appeal Fund, but very little help could be expected from that quarter: Sunday School, £6.19.4; Alms Box, £3.4.5; Fete, £29.2.3; Whist Drive, £7.9.2; Cash in Hand, £1.9.4; Balance at Bank, £68.1.8. That was barely enough to keep things going in the ordinary way—certainly, nothing to spare for an emergency of this kind.

At last she decided to tell Johnny all about it.

Johnny would know everything there was to know about such things. Perhaps he would talk to the Reverend and that would be more help than leaving it to the Major who was always cracking jokes or moaning about the woes of Ireland. Johnny's father had a big business, and when he got back home Johnny himself was going to be a business executive, and play the stock market with something called a stenographer—all of which sounded very important. Yes, she would ask Johnny and he would find a way to get the bells ringing again.

When Mr. Fedora heard that there was a chance of the Vicar leaving Merriford—and taking Mary with him—he was all for prompt action. The bleak prospect of the Vicarage in other hands did not appeal to Mr. Fedora at all. He had no doubt that things could be fixed up and a talk with the old Reverend might very well do the trick. Mr. Fedora was quite convinced that he could fill the little church to overflowing in a couple of weeks. After that the rest would be easy.

And so one evening when the Reverend was seated within his orchard, waiting for pennies to fall from Heaven, he found himself caught up in conversation with that nice young American airman who helped Mary with the garden, and had taken her to see the source of the Thames.

Mr. Fedora, having been told to be tactful, approached the topic of ecclesiastical finance by a route so circuitous that he almost lost himself in the process. He admired the Reverend's fine crop of Blenheim Oranges, now donning their Autumn livery of red and gold, and accepted the offer of a particularly splendid specimen which, he learned, would be fit for eating on Christmas Day, and not a minute before.

Having thus warmed up his engine, Mr. Fedora slipped in the clutch and drifted cautiously into a discussion concerning the church militant in the parish of Merriford. Had the broadcasting of cathedral services affected adversely the size of congregations in country districts?

The Reverend did not think so. Church attendances had declined in late years, but many causes had contributed to this unfortunate state of affairs. The absence of domestic help in upper and middle-class homes, a lack of discipline where young people were concerned, easier communications between country villages and the larger towns—all had some bearing on the problem.

What steps were the clergy taking to stop the drift?

The Vicar of Merriford considered this inquiring layman with a tolerant eye. "What steps do you suggest?" he asked.

Upon which Mr. Fedora proceeded to give him the

works. Why not apply those simple business principles that had proved successful in other fields. When a business man was faced with sales resistance, what did he do?

"What does he do?" asked the Reverend mildly.

"He doesn't sit down and take what's coming to him without putting up a fight," said the young American. "My own father started his store on a shoestring. Then, during the big slump, he nearly went broke. But where is he today? A city councilman ready to run for Congress at the next election."

"Splendid!" said the Reverend. "A real success story—and all made out of a shoestring! Do you suggest that the Church of England could overcome 'sales resistance,' I think you called it, by similar methods?"

"Sure!" said Mr. Fedora. "You've got a good article. You have to sell 'em the idea."

"Very gracious!" smiled the Reverend. "How do we begin?"

"Let the folks know you're around," said the American. "Start a Supporters' Club. Hire a guest artist. Put some pep into the sermons. Borrow a loud speaker and hop on it!"

"We seem to have been hiding our light under a bushel," said the Reverend, resignedly.

Later that evening, while weeding the Vicarage

garden, Johnny gave an account of his stewardship to Mary.

"It's okay, honey," he said. "Everything's in the bag. The business will soon be out of the red. I've softened him up and he's ready to agree to anything."

Later, when Mary took in his hot milk, the Reverend was still chuckling to himself. "Mary, my dear," he said, "never leave me alone again with that young man. No doubt he means well. . . ."

"Of course he means well," said Mary. "I hope you listened to him. What did he say?"

"Quite a lot," smiled the Reverend mischievously. "Quite a lot. He wants me to put some pep into my sermons, borrow a loud speaker and—hop on it!"

"No need to laugh at him, just because he tried to help us!" Really, Mary was most attractive when she was most indignant.

The Reverend could not resist one parting shot: "He thinks we should try to overcome the customers' sales resistance."

"Sales of what?" asked Mary.

"Shoestrings," smiled the Reverend. "I fancy he wants us to start by selling shoestrings."

It took Mary all her time to handle Johnny and the Reverend. Every evening, Johnny came along with a grand new scheme for putting Merriford on the map, but so surely as he appeared so surely did the Reverend go to ground like an old dog fox.

Even the click of the drive gate sent him scurrying up the backstairs to hide in the apple loft, and Mary had all her work cut out explaining to Johnny why he wasn't around any more.

Finally, Mr. Fedora announced that they would have to get along without him.

Having summoned a Board Meeting for the next evening, Johnny appeared with a tall, gangling youth whose lugubrious, dead-pan countenance betrayed the poker addict. "This is Walter," announced his sponsor. "The boys call him Walter because his name's Isidore. He's our Public Relations Officer. A man of few words, but give him a pen with a ball point and watch the dollars dance! Tell him about the new steeple."

"Only one?" asked the money-spinner.

"There you are," cried Mr. Fedora. "He hits the ceiling before we start. Next thing you know you'll have three steeples—one at each end and another in the middle!"

"Wouldn't one be enough?" asked Mary.

"Name your number," said Mr. Fedora, largely. "All the same to us, isn't it, Walter?"

"Sure thing," agreed the sage of golden silences.

"Give Walter the dope," explained Johnny, "and

he'll make a bill of lading read like a dime novel. Am I right, Walter?"

"Yep," said the man of few words.

And so, while Mary, spurred on by Johnny, told her plain, unvarnished tale, Walter of the dead-pan face took casual notes, warping the woof of her narrative as fancy dictated. Every now and again he would betray a faint flicker of interest in some quite irrelevant point—such as the reason why the little church stood all alone in the great field, nearly half a mile from the village. Walter, it seemed, had never heard of the Black Death, nor of the villagers who so wisely fled to higher ground, nor even of that heroic parish priest who risked his life to save his little flock.

"Tell him," urged Johnny. "Give him the real dope about this Black Death."

"People were lying in heaps or running round in circles, dying in heaps—like our rabbits last year," explained Mary.

Johnny shivered and gave her a squeeze of silent sympathy. "Where were you, honey, while all this was going on?"

17

FAR ACROSS THE SEA from the English village
of Merriford, it was press day in the editorial office of
the Pottsville *Sentinel;* and the Editor, a fat, cheerful,
Micawber of a man, sat in his shirt-sleeves wondering
where he was to find a story big enough to justify a
scare head on his leader page.

For the past week, his small corner of Texas had
been acting like the infants' class of a girls' Sunday
school. No real estate operator had gone broke and
shot himself. No shyster lawyer had grilled an erring

[141]

Congressman upon the witness stand. Even the marathon muddle in Europe offered no solution.

The Editor had gone through all his most likely galley pulls with a fine-tooth comb. He had proofs in plenty, but proofs of what? The entire issue did not amount to a hill of beans.

In desperation, he turned to the basket of manuscripts that, in his copyreader's opinion, had failed to make the grade. Very little hope there. On a poor day, such as this, no likely story was tipped onto the literary refuse dump.

The Editor flipped through pages of unpromising stuff, reading a line here and a line there. Sometimes he got no further than the heading—or the name of the author would tell him all he wanted to know. The *Sentinel* was no great organ of public opinion, but it had to angle for its readers as artfully as any New York tabloid. A scare head must be a scare head. Once a week, Pottsville had to be rocked to its very foundations—or else!

The Editor of the *Sentinel* was about to fall back on a gale disaster in Florida when his eye was caught by the title of the last article in the basket: NON-STOP FROM TEXAS. Just another of those homesick G.I.'s, he supposed, describing his personal reactions to life on a USAF Air Base in one of those nondescript foreign parts they happened to be polic-

ing at the moment. Same old story from a young airman who thought he had discovered Europe and
wanted to tell the world. . . . First American to fly the
Atlantic. . . . Non-stop, too. . . . You don't say!

Doing his three years' duty in some cockeyed corner of Wiltshire, England. Yes, there it was. All the
usual stuff. Take off from home base . . . lonely waste
of waters . . . first sight of old country, old churches,
old village pubs—Washington Irving all over again.
Why couldn't Congress bring in an Act to stop this
cruelty to Editors?

However, their might be no harm in running a sob
story once in a while. At any other time the Editor
might have crossed his fingers and counted ten, but
it was press day, his leader page was empty and that
scare head was yet to be born.

The Editor threw the manuscript at his assistant.
"Splash it across three columns," he shouted. "I know
it's lousy, but give it all you've got, and don't argue.
I know my own mind—or do I?"

Told briefly and robbed of its more lurid aspects,
the story boiled down to this:

In a strange, wild corner of Wiltshire, England,
the United States Air Force had discovered a pre-
historic settlement of Ancient Britons, so primitive
in their habits that central heating was unknown and

beds had to be thawed out nightly with warming pans.

In times of flood, the inhabitants withdrew to a range of hills known as the Cotswolds where they lived in houses with stone floors, stone roofs, and walls four feet thick. The natives were friendly but inarticulate—the most striking difference between the Cotswolds and the Catskills being that the Cotswolds had more Rip Van Winkles and they never woke up.

Their language, deriving apparently from the Gaelic, corrupted by an admixture of Urdu and Basque, was entirely incomprehensible to visitors from a more civilized country. They drove on the wrong side of the road, and their slow-moving traffic was a continual menace to Americans engaged on more urgent affairs. They were slow, too, in acquiring the finer points of western culture and always used the wrong word for everything. A funeral director was called an undertaker and a construction laborer was known as a navvy. There was no real money. . . .

The village of Merriford in which the Americans found themselves was a haunt of ancient peace, of worthy yeomen and simple peasantry, of rural repose and sheltered quiet. On Sunday mornings, when the bells in the old tower sent their sober melody across

the wet meadows, young Americans from the neighbouring Air Base joined the ruddy-faced peasants as
they moved reverently along the leafy lanes that led
to their parish church—so strangely set in the centre
of a great field, half a mile from the village.

"Such was the scene as lately as two short months
ago. Today, in his lonely vicarage, an old, tired parish
priest listens vainly for the message that will summon
his faithful flock to Evensong. For the bells of Merriford are no longer sounding across that quiet countryside, calling a pious peasantry to prayer."

Walter was getting into his stride.

"To appreciate properly the peculiar pathos of the
present situation, it is necessary to go back to the time
when a mysterious epidemic, known as the Black
Death, ravaged England. Whole villages were wiped
out; each little community was isolated in an attempt
to prevent the disease from spreading further. Those
who had the means fled to safer areas, but for the
common people there was no escape. Where they
lived they died, and where they died their bodies
were thrown into great pits, no labor being available
to provide them with individual graves.

"Merriford did not escape. Like other stricken villages it was isolated and left to its unhappy fate.
Many of the faint-hearted fled, to spread further con-

tamination throughout other smiling valleys, but a gallant remnant of stalwart yeomen, led by their devoted parish priest, stayed on to tend their dying and to bury their dead.

"With the colder weather, the epidemic died down and it was then that the genius of the heroic priest stood revealed. Leading the tragic remnant of his little flock to a position on higher ground, he bade them build their new homes amid healthier surroundings—leaving their parish church to dream alone among its green fields.

"So the quiet years slipped by, wiping out all memories of old, unhappy, far-off things. Season followed season, placid herds grazed the lush meadows, golden harvests were gathered in the fruitful Fall."

Walter was working up to his point.

"And now, suddenly, a second calamity has descended upon Merriford and its devoted priest. After a party of American engineers from the nearby Air Base had fixed a homing light to the tower of the little church, it was discovered the ancient timbers were so damaged it was no longer safe to ring the bells.

"Once again, a death-like silence has fallen over the stricken valley, and the parish priest, overwhelmed by this new disaster, wonders how he and his handful of parishioners can ever find the money to start the bells of Merriford ringing again!"

The Assistant Editor of the Pottsville *Sentinel*—a brash youth with a taste for boogie-woogie—had never heard of the Black Death and six centuries more or less meant nothing to him. It wasn't quite clear whether the United States Air Force had damaged the church tower with their new jets, or how many airmen had died of this Black Death, but time was short and he had been told not to argue. The story was certainly lousy and would take a bit of selling. He proceeded to give it the works.

Meanwhile, in the Vicarage garden, Mr. Fedora was sharing the fate of all those great business executives who fail to deliver the goods. "What," asked Mary, "has come of all your fine talk? Where is your friend Walter and those wonderful stories he promised to put in all the newspapers? Nothing yet in the Reverend's paper, or Mrs. Barrett's *News of the World,* or the parish magazine.

"What about all those dollars from rich Americans who were going to pay for a brand new belfry and three new steeples—'one at each end and another in the middle?' If this was all a joke you should be ashamed of yourselves. I don't want to see either of you again," said Mary, as she started to cry.

"Listen, honey!" pleaded Mr. Fedora. "These Rockefellers won't be rushed. They're checking up on the facts. Dallas wasn't built in a day!"

But Mary was getting frightened. The Reverend was up to something. For several days he had been writing a mysterious letter which he slipped under the blotter every time she came into the study. When, at last, she took it to the post she found that the envelope was addressed to the Bishop.

Yes, the Reverend was certainly up to something!

18

THE REVEREND was having a rare tussle with his Conscience and he was getting rather the worst of it:

"Tell me," asked Conscience, with disarming cordiality, "how is the Appeal Fund going?"

"Oh, so so!" replied the Reverend. "Only so so."

"Anywhere near your target?"

"No, I wouldn't like to say we were in sight of our target."

"By the way, what *is* your target—one thousand, two thousand."

[149]

"Approximately!" said the Reverend vaguely.

"You don't seem very clear on the financial details."

"I'm afraid finance isn't my strong point."

"You find all these figures a little bewildering?"

"Exactly!" The Reverend could have bitten his tongue out. He saw where Conscience was maneuvering him, but it was too late to retreat. "One doesn't get any younger," he added lamely.

"Ah!" said Conscience. "I was coming to that. The position of parish priest calls for more than warm sympathy and a kindly bedside manner."

"I suppose so," admitted the Vicar of Merriford.

"Especially when some unforeseen problem presents itself—death watch beetles and so on?"

"As you say," agreed the Reverend. "Death watch beetles do tend to complicate matters."

"But what are you *doing?*" pressed Conscience.

"What can I do?" asked the Reverend.

"It has been suggested you make way for a younger man," Conscience reminded him.

"That was only Mrs. Gossop—a mischievous old woman. Major O'Beirne was equally emphatic that I should remain at my post, as an act of faith. 'Practice what you preach' were his exact words."

"Anyone can produce an old proverb to prove anything," said Conscience. " '*Experientia docet,*' 'You can't put an old head on young shoulders,' and so on. After all, the Master didn't clutter up His ministry with a lot of doddering old disciples. They were labourers, artisans, fishermen in the prime of life. They toiled all day. . . ."

"And caught nothing," interjected the Reverend.

"An unworthy flippancy!"

"I admit it," sighed the Reverend, "but really, Conscience, you can be a trifle trying at times. You positively goad one into saying or doing the wrong thing. Were you ever at Monte Carlo?"

"Never!" snapped Conscience. "Quite the last place I should be likely to visit."

"The Principality has its serious side," explained the Reverend. "The Musée d'Anthropologie, and the Musée Océanographique, for instance—but I was thinking particularly of the famous exotic gardens on the Corniche with their cacti, prickly pears. . . ."

"Prickly pears!" gasped Conscience, "what in the world started you talking about prickly pears?"

"Prickly pears and prickly conscience make poor bedfellows," said the Reverend. "I haven't slept for three nights."

"You won't get rid of me by raising silly side issues," Conscience told him. "What was I saying?"

"That I should make way for a younger man," said the Reverend. "You likened me to a doddering old disciple. I take great exception to that. I may be a little short-sighted. . . ."

"Blind as a bat!" said Conscience.

"Oh, come, come, aren't you piling it on a bit?" pleaded the Reverend.

"What about that time you nearly christened one of the godfathers?" asked Conscience.

"A man isn't necessarily senile because he happens to leave his spectacles at home."

"And your memory isn't what it was. No wonder poor little Miss Robbins was upset when you inquired after her new baby."

"I was never good at names," explained the Reverend, "and, anyway, why do all these women wear the same hats?"

"Why not be honest with yourself?" asked Conscience. "Why not admit that you're getting past it? Another winter like the last one, you'll be in your coffin—and no bells tolling."

"You're very hard," sighed the Reverend.

"Of course I'm hard," said Conscience, sadly. "It's my job to be hard." And the celestial surgeon put away his scalpel, for his work was done.

About this time, the Bishop of Wessex sat down to write a letter to a parish priest in his diocese. It was a very difficult letter to write, for it involved giving pain to one who had served his church faithfully over a long period of years.

Twice the episcopal pen was dipped in the episcopal ink, and twice the ink was allowed to dry without making a mark upon the episcopal note paper. The Bishop was a kindly man and hated hurting anybody's feelings, but things were getting serious at Merriford.

"My dear Stanton," wrote the Bishop, "You will be shortly completing a ministry of fifty years in your parish. As a comparative newcomer to the Diocese, even I have been able in a short while to appreciate some of the work you have been able to do in your little community; my predecessor also spoke in glowing terms of your ministry. You have indeed, these many years, been the Persona in your parish.

"I venture to ask for your help and cooperation in a problem which in every Diocese has come to be one of priority, and not less in this one. It is a question of using the man-power of the Church of England in the very best way possible. You will have seen yourself great changes in the man-power of the Church during your long ministry. There were four thousand more clergy in the Church of England fifty years ago than there are today, and this despite a very definite increase in the population of the country."

The letter was getting more difficult as it went on:

"One way of dealing with the problem of man-power has, as you know, been used in this Diocese—that of linking up parishes, thus creating a united benefice from two or three separate parishes with a single incumbent. This has not always been popular, and is a blow to the parochial system of the Church of England, which many feel is its great strength. But the shortage of clergy is so serious that it is no longer possible to place a clergyman in every country parish, and owing to the changes in the value of money, it is impossible for him to live on the endowments of a single parish.

"All this I know you are well aware of," continued the Bishop, "but the problem actually concerns your own parish of Merriford. As you know, the parish next to yours is now vacant, and the Patron tells me he has had no success in finding anyone to take it, largely on account of the poorness of the living. My Pastoral Committee have recommended that this parish and yours when the time comes, shall be joined, thus forming a united benefice. I believe I could find the right man to tackle these two parishes almost at once, if both parishes were united."

Why did parish priests grow old and why must Bishops be faced with such painful decisions?

"In view of this, and bearing in mind the vacant parish next door, would you consider giving up your work in your parish? I do so appreciate what a wrench this would be to you, but fifty years is a long time, and perhaps one of the most difficult lessons we have to learn is to know when to hand over our work to others.

"Will you think this over? It will not, I know, be a popular move to join the two parishes, but you, with your local knowledge of the people, could do much to pave the way."

The letter concluded with a brief reference to the root of the trouble: "I have heard with concern the adverse report on the Church Fabric, and I know you will do all you can, locally, to raise money for repair work. It is not feasible that so small a community should carry the whole burden. I expect we can make a Diocesan Grant, and it is possible that the Ancient Monuments people might help, and the C.P.R.E. and the Warneford Trust."

But the Bishop held out no false hopes: "If, after reflection, you do decide to give up your present living, I should be most happy to license you as a Preacher in the Diocese, and I have little doubt that you would find many calls on your time. Your friend and Bishop, John Wessex."

The letter was never sent. The Bishop of Wessex had barely signed his firm but kindly epistle when the afternoon post brought him an envelope bearing the Merriford postmark:

"My dear Bishop," wrote the Reverend, "I have felt for some time that the work of even such a small country parish as this is getting a little beyond me. I had hoped to complete fifty years in the service of the church but, in view of the special effort now demanded, I feel that it would be unfair to you and to my successor to let my personal feelings prejudice an already difficult situation. I will not pretend that this letter has been an easy one to write, but it would have been far more painful for me to have received a kindly reminder that a man is no younger than his arteries and that faith without works is dead . . . I place myself in your hands, and beg to remain. . . ."

Conscience, it is said, makes cowards of us all, but Conscience had for once made a hero who was not afraid to burn his boats.

UP AT THE AIR BASE—that aloof, mysterious world of Nissen huts and three-mile runways—the United States Air Force carried on with its self-imposed task of saving the world for democracy.

In the lounge of the Officers Club the Base Commander and some of his officers were sitting around in an unofficial get-together, sorting out all those tremendous trifles that complicate life in a service com-

[157]

munity, and winnowing the wheat of legitimate grievance from the chaff of idle complaint. Coffee had been served and the Club Officer, a cheerful type, had defended that dubious beverage with a heat his coffee certainly did not possess. But there was nothing really wrong with it. This was just a traditional opening gambit which set the tone for what followed.

Among the senior officers and executives present might be noted the Chaplain, Doctor, Information Officer, Education Officer, Projects Officer—each ready to hold the baby for his Department if need arose.

The Base Commander fixed his Chaplain with a cold, blue eye. "Well Chaplain," he said, "what story of sin and shame have *you* got to tell?"

The Chaplain, a veteran of two wars and now rising thirty, grinned happily. "Sir," he replied, "I would not sully your innocent ears with details of my unpleasant activities."

"But, Chaplain," protested the Commander, "my young and innocent ears are itching to hear the facts of life. What *did* happen on Tuesday night in Sheepscombe Bottom?"

It should, perhaps, be explained that one of the Chaplain's varied duties was to supervise the love affairs of the Base and to suggest possible adjustments where maladjustment reared its ugly head. He, it was, who vetted the backgrounds of contracting parties contemplating matrimony and explored the situation when eager youth anticipated the nuptial knot. The apochryphal happening in Sheepscombe Bottom, the local lovers' lane, was merely a fly thrown over likely water in hope of a rise.

"What you need, Chaplain," continued the C.O., "is the advice of an older and more experienced man. Get the Information Officer to turn a few pages of his horrid past."

After this bit of badinage the session got down to business—nothing very outstanding, but all very vital to the comfort and happiness of the Base. Then came a further onslaught and, once again, the Chaplain was on the hot seat.

"Oh, by the way, Chaplain," said the Commander, "I've had a rather serious complaint about your department. Mrs. Gossop regrets. . . ."

He was interrupted by a roar of laughter. Every one of the officers present had received a letter from Mrs. Gossop regretting this or that, and "Mrs. Gossop regrets" had become a catchword in the Club. What was Mrs. Gossop regretting this time?

"Mrs. Gossop regrets," continued the Chairman, "that a perfectly reasonable protest addressed to the Chaplain was received in a spirit of levity and 'called forth a facetious, even impudent reply quite out of keeping with his sacred office.' How are you going to wriggle out of that one, Chaplain?"

"Sorry, sir!" replied the contrite Chaplain. "Mrs. Gossop complained that a local girl, 'notorious for associating with the lowest type of American service-man,' spent half-an-hour on her front porch with a young airman. Mrs. Gossop wanted to know what this young airman, a mere boy, was doing on her front porch at that time of night. I referred her to the Information Officer—didn't I, Steve?"

"You did," replied the Information Officer. "I forgot to thank you."

"Don't worry," said the Chaplain. "We pass through this world but once—anything we can do to cheer things up a bit. . . ."

"Am I to understand," asked the Base Commander, "that my Information Officer was the young airman standing on Mrs. Gossop's front porch, necking with a doubtful character?"

"Oh dear, no, Sir!" replied the Chaplain.

"Then why drag *him* into it?"

"Because, Sir," replied the Chaplain, "I felt that I needed the advice of an older and more experienced man."

Thanks to his pulpit training and constant wres-tlings with the Powers of Darkness, the Chaplain could wriggle out of most situations. None knew this better than his old wartime buddy and present commanding officer.

"Much more of this, Chaplain," he said, "and I'll have you and Steve swap jobs for keeps. He would preach a better sermon."

"Colonel," was the reply, "make the transfer operative by five o'clock today and I'll be the happiest man on the Base!"

"Why five o'clock?" asked the Colonel.

"At five o'clock," said the Chaplain, "I have a date with an airman, 3rd class, who will be twenty years old come Sunday. He wants to marry the daughter of a local dirt farmer, aged eighteen. I will ask him if he has written to his folks back home and he will say, 'What's the use? They don't understand.' I will then inquire whether the girl friend has told *her* folks the glad tidings and he will say, 'What's the use? They don't understand, either.'

"I will next invite him to show financial responsibility for a wife by producing $900 to cover her passage to the States and the cost of setting up a home. When I have loosened the collar of his ball jacket and he has revived somewhat, I will explain that when he is promoted to Staff Sergeant he gets free transport home for his wife, and need produce only 300 bucks from his bill fold as financial responsibility.

"Cheered up somewhat, he will ask when this glad

day may be hoped to arrive and I will explain how I once heard of an airman 3rd class who became airman 2nd class in five months, airman 1st class in another eight months and staff sergeant in twelve months. He will ask how many months all those months make added together and when I tell him he will say, sorry, but there are reasons why they can't wait that long.

"He will then ask me to lend him the $900. . . ."

"All right, Chaplain, you win!" laughed the Base Commander, and the conversation proceeded to a discussion of such vexed questions as the prohibitive tariff for the insurance of American servicemen's cars in England and the exorbitant charges for apartments demanded from married officers living off the Base.

The last item for consideration was the celebration of Thanksgiving Day in two or three weeks' time. There was to be a ceremonial parade, followed by street dancing in the big square to which the general public would be invited.

The Bishop of Wessex would bless the feast; the Base Commander would deliver his usual address on Anglo-American Relations from a Flat Bed drawn up against the wall of the new Service Club; the Base band would play "Deep in the Heart of Texas" and the onlookers would join in spontaneous chorus. They planned to make it a real slap-up Texas Day with flocks of turkeys from Forth Worth, ten-gallon Stetsons from Dallas, and a load of bright cowboy shirts from Houston to add to the fun.

Stands would be erected on two sides of the square and the Base Commander ran his finger down a list of V.I.P.'s invited to occupy them: the local J.P., the doctor, parish officials—even Mrs. Gossop, if only to protect them from that lady's regrets at a later date.

"What about the parson?" asked the Commander.

"He'd come with his Bishop," said the Chaplain.

"Better send him a separate invitation," advised the Commander. "I'm not up in this diocesan drill but I'd hate to hurt his feelings—he's a nice guy."

The party was breaking up when an orderly handed the Colonel a letter bearing all the outward trappings of extreme urgency and expressed by every device known to the postal authorities. The Base Commander opened it, read it through twice and then called to the Doctor.

"Doc!" he said, "why wasn't I told about this?"

"This what, Sir?"

"This epidemic!"

"Epidemic?" exclaimed the bewildered doctor. "We've had no epidemic—apart from the usual sporadic outbreak of lunacy among the fly boys and that isn't contagious."

"Somebody's mad," said the Commander. "It says here . . ."

"Mrs. Gossop regrets!" whispered a sepulchral voice.

"No, boys! This is serious," snapped the Colonel, as he proceeded to read from the mysterious document:

"The writer has heard with the deepest sorrow of the twin disasters that have fallen upon the village of Merriford, Wilts., England. She refers to the epidemic which has cost so many lives and the collapse of the belfry in the tower of the Parish Church. While the dead cannot be brought to life, it is surely the duty of all right-thinking Americans to rally round the heroic parish priest and repair the damage apparently due to the negligence of the U.S.A.F. and their modern engines of war. The writer, who is of British descent, begs to inclose a small draft which she places at the disposal of the Base Commander, to be applied at his absolute discretion to the immediate repair of the church tower. 'Come all to church, good people!' Signed: A Daughter of Texas."

The reader paused to let the effect of this odd communication sink in.

"Any address?" asked someone.

"Only the postmark," explained the Commander. "Anyone heard of Pottsville?"

"Search me!" said the Information Officer.

"Referred to Education!" suggested the Chaplain.

"More like a case for Doc," countered the Education Officer.

"Sounds like a poor sort of joke to me," said Doc.

"She's prepared to pay for her fun," the Colonel reminded him. "Any other suggestions?"

"They've been having some trouble with the church tower," said the Chaplain. "Something wrong with the timbers. Haven't been able to ring the bells for weeks."

"When my boys were fixing the light on the steeple," began the Projects Officer.

The Base Commander was not one to lose his sleep over trifles. He had a new Wing flying in next morning and time was short.

"Okay, boys," he said. "We'll tie it up with Thanksgiving Day. Get the old parson along, and I'll toss him across the small donation at the right moment. Now, get out, all of you before somebody else starts something."

"What about the epidemic?" asked Doc.

"Bats in the Belfry," said the Commander. "A purely ecclesiastical complaint. Passed to Chaplain for necessary action."

"How about this suggestion that we were responsible for damage to the tower?" asked the Projects Officer.

"Could be," said the Commander. "Once your clumsy lot get started there's no telling what might happen. Rig them up a temporary support to keep their bells going till they get them ringing good and proper."

"On what authority?" asked the Projects Officer, a stickler for procedure who had never yet been known to laugh himself to death.

The Base Commander had heard enough. "Here's your authority," he said:

" 'The Commanding Officer, fearing that the absence of church bells may affect the morale of personnel at Merriford Air Base, hereby instructs the Projects Officer to install a temporary structure which will permit the said bells to be rung for the greater glory of God, the United States of America, and those details of the U.S.A.F. under his immediate command . . .' "

"And if they won't let us into the church?" persisted the Projects Officer.

"I'll ring up the Bishop," said the Commander. "You'll have a special dispensation by the morning."

"You see, Bishop," explained the voice of the Base Commander on the episcopal telephone, "our boys

like to hear a lot of loud, cheerful noise, and everyone's getting the willies since the church bells stopped
ringing. You're very kindly coming along to bless
the feast of Thanksgiving Day, and we would consider it an appropriate gesture if you would allow us
in return to run up a temporary structure that would
permit the bells to get going again. Okay?"

To say that the Bishop of Wessex was dumb-
founded was one of those understatements. He was,
in fact, knocked all of a heap. "But why," he asked,
"why should we be indebted to you for this extraor-
dinary kindness?"

The Base Commander, having acted on sudden
impulse, was at a bit of a loss to justify his good
intentions. "Well, Bishop," he explained, "we like
that old padre of yours down in the village. Anyhow,
it's only a temporary job—not worth talking about.
Just a couple of girders to keep the bells from falling,
till you can get down to it. We'll start in right away."

"I'm afraid there's more to it than you think,"
said the Bishop. "Those old timbers. . . ."

The Base Commander laughed. "Bishop, we move
mountains. If you want the church brought up to
the village, or the village moved down to the church,
only say the word."

The telephone does not lend itself to protracted
argument. In the end, the Bishop agreed to a prelimi-

nary investigation which might provide the basis for a subsequent decision. Such is the English way. . . . The Base Commander instructed his Projects Officer to hop on it. The thing was as good as done.

The Reverend, for his part, was a little bewildered by the sudden arrival of a working party from the Air Base. But he had been expecting a further official investigation and this, he supposed, was it. He handed over his spare set of keys and hoped for the best.

THE MORNING of Thanksgiving Day was bright
and not too cold—one of those rare days when November shows us what she can do in the way of
weather if she really tries.

At the Vicarage, Mary was in a state of suppressed
excitement for the Bishop would be coming to tea
after visiting the Air Base, and she was wearing her
new nylons for the great occasion.

The first thing was to get the Reverend to the
Thanksgiving ceremony in time. Mary had been on

her knees half the night—polishing the floors and washing the stone passages—and in the kitchen baking cakes all the morning. Now she had to see that neither of them looked like something that had been pulled out of a rag-bag. So the Reverend's shoes were polished until they shone like his study floor, and the new nylons were pulled and patted until they did credit to Mary's nice pair of legs.

The Reverend would be started off in good time because he didn't like to be hurried, and Mary would follow later when she had laid the table, made up the fires and taken the cakes out of the oven.

Now, they were standing together in the sunshine, on the Vicarage drive, taking final stock of one another. The Reverend certainly paid for a bit of looking after—wonderful old man for his age, with that fine old face and that nice, kind twinkle in his eye. Mary was quite proud of him. He would stand up to any of them—Colonels or no Colonels—Bishops or no Bishops.

And what of Mary? The last few months had certainly done something to Mary! From being a little scrap of a thing, she had blossomed out into a young woman worthy of any airman's wolf whistle; while there was about her an air of distinction that made her stand out from all the other village girls. That was especially true today when a little excitement lent a touch of color to her cheeks; and a pair of new nylons gave her that bit of extra confidence they always give to a girl wearing them for the first time.

The scene at the Air Base was a real thrill for the country people crowding in from the little villages. There was a great welcome arch over the entrance. Military police, who would usually have been checking passes, were handing out free programs to all comers. Each child as it came through was given a bag of candies. A large, cheerful M.P. even handed one of these to Mary.

"Here y'are, baby," he laughed.

She wandered past the snack bars with their hot dogs and hamburgers, through the carnival ground, across to the stands, already packed to bursting. And here, again, Cinderella found a fairy prince who had kept a spare seat for just such a case as this. He may have looked like a rather ordinary airman but he had the magic password. "Come right in," he smiled, with an engaging drawl. "Come right in. We've been holding up the show till you were safely parked. See you in the intermission, honey!"

Mary looked round the parade square to see what had happened to the Reverend. On the platform, the Base band was playing lively swing music instead of the usual military marches and Gilbert and Sullivan selections. Behind them were ranged all the notables of the district, with a row of empty seats for the Commanding Officer and his personal friends. Her eyes searched anxiously, down each row and along the surrounding stands, but no Reverend was to be seen.

And then she found him, perched away at the end of the back row, a solitary little black spot, looking as lonely as an old crow on the top of an elm tree. Mary was furious. If *that* was all they thought of him he would have been better at home. It might have been his own fault; he had probably slipped in quietly and nobody knew he was there, but *someone* might have kept a lookout for him. After all, he *was* the Vicar.

But the band had stopped playing and were moving off the platform to take up their position at the head of the parade. The empty chairs were being brought to the front of the reviewing stand and young officers were filling them with the privileged V.I.P.'s for whom they had been reserved.

The Base Commander was talking to his Chaplain who was standing in a little group with the Bishop. He seemed worried about something, and they were all looking around as though they had lost somebody.

A minute later, the Chaplain was up in the back row persuading the Reverend to come down and sit next to the Bishop, among the great ones of the world—where he rightly belonged. Mary could now relax. She settled down to enjoy herself.

Johnny had warned her he wouldn't be around until after the parade. That wouldn't be long now. The band was getting ready to lead the march. Mary fairly shivered with excitement. This was the first ceremonial parade she had seen and she hadn't the least idea what to expect. For all she knew Johnny might be riding on a white horse, carrying a drawn sword.

Here they came! First the band, then the officers—and then Johnny. True, it was a bit of a job picking him out from all those other airmen, but when they swung past the platform and the Commanding Officer took the salute, it was all very wonderful. How well they marched and how smart they looked, especially Johnny! Once again, Mary was able to relax and give herself up to happy daydreams in the bright November sunshine.

The Colonel's speech—the usual one on better Anglo-American relations—was a great success. He admitted the difficulty of setting up huge military establishments in another country in peace-time, but now that Americans had learned not to talk to strangers in railway carriages, everything was going along fine. Indeed, the conservative Britisher was beginning to adopt some of their strange American customs and he looked forward to the day when he would meet his old friend, the Vicar of Merriford, complete with blue jeans, windbreaker and a "crew cut."

And then, suddenly, as though joining in the laughter, the bells of Merriford church started to ring again. The Americans, having finished their job, had smuggled in ringers from surrounding villages without a soul being any the wiser. A watcher, placed on the tower, had passed down a signal from the Air Base, and the Great Surprise, so happily conceived, so beautifully timed, was complete. The bells of Merriford were ringing again.

The effect was indescribable—almost as though the gates of some celestial Festival Hall had swung open and all the angels had started singing.

Everybody was looking at the Reverend—who was looking at his Bishop—who was looking at the Base Commander—who was laughing.

"You young rascal!" whispered the Bishop. "How did you manage it in the time?"

"Sorry, Bishop," said the Base Commander. "Thanksgiving Day! We must have our little joke! Go ahead, it's all yours."

The Bishop rose from his seat and stood for a moment listening to the bells. Everybody was listening to the bells. As someone said later at the Thatchers Arms, you could have heard a pin drop in a haystack. Finally, the Bishop spoke.

"In our more idle moments," he said, "we tell one another that the Age of Miracles is past. When we talk like this we are apt to forget our American friends with us on this platform. When I suggest that Americans can perform miracles, I am not referring specifically to the lovely old legends of the Saints, nor to supernatural events recorded in Old or New Testament history. I am thinking, rather, of the kind of physical or material miracle we have just been enjoying.

"But at the back of every miracle, secular or spiritual, there must be a motive worthy of the wonder which it creates—and the motive behind this modern Miracle of Merriford, as I am not afraid to call it, must be apparent to all. It is prompted by kindliness, good neighborliness, and, I dare to hope, appreciation for any small services our people have been able to render to you who were, at one time, strangers within our gates.

"Speaking for my old friend here, his parishioners and myself, I can only say how deeply grateful we are to you, sir, and to all who may have been concerned in this happy gesture of goodwill. We thank you!"

"Ladies and Gentlemen," said the Base Commander, "your Bishop forgot to remind you that this little renovation my boys rigged up is strictly temporary in character. Any time, in the next two hundred years, you're liable to run up against the same trouble, and, as it's as well to be on the safe side, I'm handing to your padre here a small draft, from an anonymous Texas well-wisher, to get him out of the red when that time comes."

Upon which, the band struck up: "Deep in the Heart of Texas" and Mary hurried off to join her Johnny who was waiting for her in the heart of the fair.

The Americans certainly did things in a big way. Never in the history of Merriford had there been such a celebration. Cold buffets were ranged all round the parade ground and old Reuben discovered a barrel of free beer which kept him busy for the rest of the afternoon. If this was Thanksgiving Day, the sooner England had something to give thanks for the better!

In the big dining hall, the nobility, gentry, and anyone who could crowd onto that particular band wagon sat down to the traditional Thanksgiving banquet of turkey, cranberry sauce, sweet potatoes, giblet gravy and corn; this was followed by pumpkin pie, whipped cream, nuts, candies, and fresh fruits. The afternoon was well advanced when the Reverend and his Bishop found themselves sitting over the big fire in the study of the old Vicarage.

They talked comfortably of the events of that eventful day; and all the time the Reverend was waiting for the kindly words that would mark the close of his ministry. He had had no answer to his letter but this, surely, was the setting for the final scene. . . . Any minute now. Well, he wouldn't feel the hurt of parting so desperately as he might have done. He wouldn't be leaving Merriford as a complete failure.

But still the Bishop couldn't seem to bring himself to start upon the painful subject. He kept shying away from it, talking instead of the wonderful organization and discipline at the Air Base; the pleasant personality of the young Chaplain; the quiet humour of the Commanding Officer—until the Reverend could bear the suspense no longer.

"You got my letter, Bishop?" he asked.

"Letter! What letter?" asked the Bishop, still deep in the heart of Texas.

"My letter of resignation," explained the Reverend.

"Oh, *that!*" said the Bishop. "My *dear* fellow!" and he waved the unpleasant topic away as a matter of so little importance that it would not bear discussion.

"I felt you might be thinking that the time had

come for me to hand over the living to a younger man."

The Bishop leaned forward and warmed his hands before the cheerful blaze. "Yes," he said at last, "I got your letter, but after the way you handled that difficult problem of the church bells . . ."

"After the way *I* handled it," gasped the Reverend.

"I found myself wondering what might have happened if we *had* handed over the parish to that younger man."

"But, Bishop, I had nothing whatever to do with it."

"These things don't just happen," said the Bishop.

"I assure you, I hadn't the slightest idea."

"No one more surprised than the striker," smiled the Bishop, who had played a bit of tennis in his younger days. "Then why do you suppose the Americans acted as they did? Something you've forgotten, perhaps."

"My memory isn't what it was," admitted the Reverend.

"Forget you wrote that letter," said the Bishop. "Unless, of course, you really want to go. Why not stay on and see the job finished? They gave you something to start your Appeal Fund."

"Dear me!" sighed the Reverend. "There I go, forgetting again. Now where did I put it?" A crumpled piece of paper fell from his handkerchief, and the Bishop, reaching down, picked it up from the floor.

"Every little helps," he said, smoothing it out on his knee. "Now where are my glasses . . . Why, bless my soul, what's this? Well, I . . . Well . . . Well, really! This is too much!"

"Oh dear," cried the Reverend, "what have I done now?"

The Bishop smiled. "I'm afraid I nearly forgot myself," he said, "but the provocation was great. How much is ten thousand dollars in real money?"

21

IT WAS a White Christmas of dry snow and bright sunshine with all the bells ringing. What the Bishop had not been afraid to describe as the Miracle of Merriford had proved a nine days' wonder, almost forgotten, but it was inevitable that this season of the bells should set all the tongues wagging again.

How dreadful if there had been no bells for Christmas! Fancy all that money coming from nowhere—closing the Appeal Fund as soon as it was opened. They did say one of those American millionaires. . . .

The mystery had never been properly cleared up. Some said one thing and some said another, but it was all a tangle of loose ends. None of the clues seemed to lead anywhere, possibly because the parties concerned had their own reasons for lying low and saying nothing.

Nothing more had been heard of the eccentric donor. "A Daughter of Texas," having done good by stealth would apparently have blushed to find it fame.

The Base Commander was thankful to see the end of the whole business and didn't give it a second thought.

The Bishop was frankly bewildered.

So was the Reverend.

Sweetly the bells, *ding-dong, ding-dong,* rang out across the quiet valley. Everyone went to Church on Christmas morning. There would be the decorations to look at; the choir would walk in procession from the west door, and the carols were always worth listening to. Even Major O'Beirne slipped into a corner of the Vicarage pew and Mrs. Gossop donned the forgotten finery of ancient days.

During the weeks following Thanksgiving Day, quite a lot of Americans from the Base had started to attend morning service at the parish church; so

THE MIRACLE OF MERRIFORD

that, in one way and another, the Reverend was faced
with an overflowing congregation, as he climbed the
pulpit steps, to deliver a very abbreviated address
that would permit his parishioners to get the turkeys
out of their ovens in time for their Christmas din-
ners.

Mary had warned him that their own turkey—
mysteriously arrived from America—would be done
to a turn by half-past twelve and not a minute later.
If he talked too long she would never forgive him.
The Reverend smiled as a fugitive little memory
fluttered in the back of his mind. What was it that
odd young man had said? "Hop on it!" Yes, that was
it. Very well, he would hop on it.

Back at the Vicarage, he found to his surprise that
the table was laid for three. Mary had invited the
young airman to share their Christmas dinner. Very
thoughtful of her. These boys would be lonely up at
the Air Base. Perhaps he should have mentioned
that in his sermon. How forgetful of him. . . .

The dinner was a great success. Mr. Fedora carved,
and told them how turkeys ran about in Texas like
chickens on an English farm. There was a place called
Sweet Valley—when he had finished his three years'
service he was going to get him a wife and together
they would run a turkey farm to supply the British

[185]

market. Was the Vicar of Merriford ever in Sweet Valley?

No, the Reverend had never been in Sweet Valley. A pretty name! He would like to go there some day.

Mr. Fedora promised him that his wish should be gratified. He should certainly come to Sweet Valley. There would always be an apartment waiting for him.

"Rather an expensive trip," smiled the Reverend.

"Trip, nothing!" said Mr. Fedora. "Once you're there, you'll be there for keeps."

The Reverend was getting frightened. What was this dynamic young man up to now?

"Before you've been there five minutes," said Mr. Fedora, "you'll be so settled in, they won't shift you from Sweet Valley with a bulldozer. Think it over. There's no hurry. Loads of time to get used to the idea. Just you and me—and Miss Mary!"

"A second exodus," smiled the Reverend. "But suppose Merriford can't get along without us? We mustn't let you make all these arrangements and then find. . . ."

Mr. Fedora brushed these trivial difficulties to one side. Three years was a long time. Not to worry. Not to meet trouble halfway. Anything could happen in three years.

The Reverend played his last card: "But, Mary,

[186]

wouldn't you be afraid of all those turkeys?" he asked.

"No!" said Mary. "I shouldn't be frightened. If I can manage you two men, I could surely manage a few turkeys!"